MARK TWAIN
ON THE MOON

Book Two: The Deirdre

by

Michael Schulkins

Other books by Michael Schulkins

Beltway

Mother Lode

Sting Suite

Up a Tree: A Jobs and Plunkitt Galactic Adventure

Book Two: The Deirdre

Prologue

You hold before you the second volume of an extended work describing my adventures, tribulations, and occasional successes on the Moon. The first volume, Mark Twain on the Moon Book 1: Prospectors! tells the story of how I set off to prospect for water ice and precious metals in the lonely craters and desolate mountains of the Lunar wilderness, and how an untimely death seemed the only reward that might await me there.

In case you have forgotten the particulars, Book 1 details how my future mining partner Calvin Bemis and I earned our grub stake working as "pickers", or the low men on the totem pole at Lunar Consolidated Mines. After getting chewed up and spat out by an immense strip-mining machine called Baby, we left the picking business, bought a marvelous great digging leviathan we nicknamed the Beast, a small mountain of prospecting gear and supplies, and an overpriced map directing us to a promising crater. We dubbed it Farley's Crater in honor of the amiable swindler who had sold us the map, and when we reached it, we promptly got ourselves and the Beast trapped in a sea of Moon dust, with rapidly dwindling supplies, and little to no hope of being rescued before our air ran out.

But, as I revealed at the end of that volume, Calvin and I did not die—not quite. And the reason we didn't—detailed in this volume—was the timely intervention of the men of the Deirdre. Their story, which became inextricably entwined with our own, is related here.

Chapter One

I was awakened by a persistent buzzing noise.
Well, I thought, still three-quarters asleep, now a fly
has got into the cabin. Fleas we had aplenty, but the
presence of a fly was a novelty. How had it got in?
There must be a hole in the screen door, or had I
forgotten to shut the airlock? A fly might enjoy the
Moon, while he lasted—what with the paltry
gravitation, he might get by without flapping his
wings but once or twice a week. This deep thinking
finally brought me awake, more or less, and after a
minute I roused Bemis.

"Cal," I croaked, "what is that infernal buzzing
noise? Do you think you could shut it off so I can die
in peace?"

"What?" he groaned. Then all of a sudden he was
shouting. "Sam! Sam, wake up. We're saved! We're
saved, I tell you! That's the incoming signal indicator
on the radio. Somebody heard our S.O.S. and they're
calling back." He reached across to the radio controls
and turned on the receiver.

The radio's speaker crackled with static for a
moment, then I heard a voice calling, "Ahoy, the
digger. Ahoy in there." Then, "Booger! I hope they
aren't dead already. Ahoy, the digger! Do you hear
me?"

7

Bemis called back immediately. "Yes! Yes, we hear you quite clearly. Thank God you heard us. We thought we were dead for sure. We're in a large crater buried in Moon dust up to our ears. Is there any way you can help us?"

"Fear not, mate," said the voice. "I know where you're situated. I can see you from here, or leastways what's left sticking out of the dust. You're in the soup pretty deep a'right, but we'll rouse you out. Should be alongside in just a few minutes."

"What?" said Bemis. "Do you mean you're in the crater? Where are you?"

"Of course I'm in the crater, ya silly booger, else I couldn't be talking to you, could I?" He mumbled, "Greenhorns sure enough," then added, "You can probably see us by now. We're off your port beam. Go and look out the window on the left side."

As someone who had piloted a steamboat or two in my otherwise misspent youth, I felt an impulse to inform our savior that I for one knew the difference between port and starboard, but as that was slightly less urgent than being saved from certain death, I decided to let it go. There was no man on Earth, or I should say, no man in the Moon, to whom I would less wish to give offense.

We both stuck our noses against the indicated viewport and strained to see something, anything, in the sea of dust. We hadn't the slightest idea what we were looking for, but then it didn't matter. Anyone or anything would be welcome—Valkyries in a winged chariot, a horde of red Indians in a birchbark canoe, anything—welcomed like the prodigal son carrying a golden goose in the holy grail.

"I think I see something." Bemis pointed out the port. "Over there."

Finally I saw what he'd found. I detected it first by the fireworks, distant as they were, then as a disturbance in, or above, the dust, in the form of two plumes rising above the surface, curving in broad low arcs that shone with an eerie greenish scintillating glow, despite the light from the waning Earth. The dust did not float in a cloud above the surface, but rose and fell in two neat, sparkling parabolas, both advancing toward us at a steady pace.

"We see you! We see you!" cried Bemis.

"Fine," our savior replied. "I'll be coming up abeam of you in a minute. How are you fixed for air?"

"We can still breathe for the moment," Calvin admitted, "but I fear all of our air cylinders are exhausted."

"Very well," he said. "I expect you'll not expire before we can get you to the Deirdre. But you'll need to be in your pressure gear for a short while once we get there. There be two of you, from what I can see. I'll send a man across with two cylinders of air. And I'll send over some water. I expect you'll be needing that as well."

"Yes. Thank you. That would be, uh—" Bemis looked at me.

"Splendid," I said.

"That would be splendid," he said.

It sounded as if our benefactor was far more ready to effect our rescue than we were to receive it. That makes sense, I suppose. No one in his right mind plans to be rescued, because no one in his right mind plans to get himself into enough trouble to need it.

As our rescuer approached, I was able to make out some features of his conveyance. Sadly, it was not a winged chariot chock-full of Valkyries, but then it was not red Indians either, so I was satisfied.

"That's the strangest-looking craft I've ever seen," Calvin said.

Indeed, the vehicle, vessel, whatever it was, was unique in my experience, and perhaps that was inevitable, as it was clearly constructed with the unique environment of Farley's Crater in mind. I wanted to call it a boat, just to be done with it, or a traction engine, or a Fourth of July parade float (albeit one lacking bunting and the inevitable advertisement for the local haberdasher on its stern), but I found that I could not, as it had the salient characteristics of all three—something like the celebrated Sphinx of Giza, which has the body of a lion, the head of a man, and the disposition of a librarian. At the center of the thing was a steam-powered tractor, with its pilot's seat and tiller situated behind the boiler, open to the vacuum. Behind the tractor came a sort of wheeled platform—this was the parade float part—where two men were already taking a pair of air cylinders from an aluminum rack. All this, if not exactly Company issue, was not too far out of the ordinary. It was what surrounded the tractor and the parade float that made the craft unique, and useful in Farley's Crater. An enormous wedge of sheet aluminum, something like a cow catcher on a locomotive only larger and far more comprehensive, made up the prow of the vessel —but did not stop there, not by a long shot. The great sloping wedge continued along the sides of the craft until it had wrapped itself completely around both the tractor and the parade float, and closed up again behind them. The whole construction looked something like the hull of an ocean-going ship, only turned upside down and with the bottom torn out. That is, it looked something like that, but fortunately not much.

"Yes," I agreed, "but it appears to be effective. If we'd thought to bring along some sheet aluminum, we might not be in this pickle." As the craft came on, the wedge-shaped prow cut through the dust as if it were water. However, it did not float upon the dust like a proper boat but simply shoved it aside with its great cow catcher, leaving the traction engine and parade float to roll along in a dust-free cavity inside. Once it had slowed to come alongside, the rooster tails of shimmering Moon dust subsided, but a sort of wake of glowing, discommoded dust could still be seen beyond the stern.

A minute later the "dust boat," as I'd decided to christen the thing, came abreast of us, and we put on our helmets and prepared to leave the digger, likely for the last time. As much as I'd wished, not to say yearned, lusted, maybe even prayed to be rescued, it seemed a shame to abandon the Beast. It seemed wrong to leave it there to, well, not rust exactly, as that would require the presence of air, but nevertheless to sit there up to its airlock in Moon dust, silent, idle, useless, and forlorn, like a 'coon dog too old to hunt, or a politician too honest to graft, if there is such a thing. It seemed to me wasteful, thoughtless, callous, even cruel to leave it behind, but after all it was only a dumb piece of machinery. A piece of machinery as close to our hearts as our livers, I'll admit, but still nothing compared to a living, breathing thing like a good 'coon dog, or a wife. Still, I couldn't help the way I felt at that moment, and I knew Calvin felt it as well. Nevertheless, he radioed that we were ready to go.

Before I had managed to wedge myself into the Dutch oven, however, our benefactor called back, saying, "Hold on there, ya boogers. Don't be in such a hurry to abandon ship. Are you towing anything behind that digger?"

"Well, there is a sled," Bemis said.

"Of course you are," said our deliverer. "That's part 'n' parcel of why you're stuck."

"Yes," Bemis answered, "but we're going to have to leave it behind with the digger. There's no way to get it free."

"Waste not, want not, gentlemen. I expect the Deirdre can use some of the cargo you're carrying."

"But it belongs—" Bemis started.

"Quiet, Calvin," I said. "He can have the lot for all I care. It seems a reasonable price to pay for saving our lives, don't you think?"

Bemis nodded his head. "We tried going into the dust to save some of it," he said into the speaking cone, "but we weren't too successful."

"And it cost us a parcel of air into the bargain," I added.

"Never mind. You just sit tight," our deliverer said. "Leave the salvaging to us."

I said, "I thought you wanted us to come over there to, what's it called, the Deirdre."

A chuckle came out of the radio speaker. "No, this ain't the Deirdre, it's only the dust boat. You stay where you are. There'll be plenty enough for you to do once we get you out of the soup."

The dust boat—I felt some satisfaction that I'd gotten its moniker right—came alongside, or within a half-dozen yards of us, and immediately a man in a pressure suit leapt from the parade float and flew across the space between us, carrying two cylinders of air, which he placed beside the hatch of the Dutch oven. It was a prodigious leap at that distance, even by the Moon's extravagant standards, and a moment later the other man did it too, this time carrying what I correctly presumed to be a large container of water. He cranked open the outer hatch of the airlock and the first man placed the containers inside. I wasted no time in putting the airlock through its paces, and we had fresh air and water once again.

Apart from the fact that their efforts were in service of the noblest of goals, namely our salvation, it was a pleasure to watch those men operate in the Lunar environment, especially in the peculiar conditions served up by Farley's Crater. They moved through the vacuum with the effortless grace and ruthless efficiency of a ballet dancer, a trapeze artist, or a three-card Monte entrepreneur cleaning out suckers in Central Park. Although I have rightly warned the oxygen-drunk greenhorns and starry-eyed excursionists among you against the hazards of leaping about on the Moon's surface, a skilled practitioner can accomplish much in this line with reasonable safety, and watching those men jump easily and precisely between dust boat and digger with their arms full of containers, and in general gambol about like a pair of tomcats at a cotillion, was a convincing demonstration of their mastery of this dangerous and demanding art.

By comparison, Bemis and I would surely have found ourselves floating face down in the dust soon after attempting such feats, or worse, found ourselves lying toes up in the morgue. Any acquaintance Bemis and I had with Lunar acrobatics must necessarily come from our time served as pickers. To be sure, picking teaches one how to survive and endure in a pressure suit on the Moon's surface, but precious little else, and amateur terpsichore is expressly forbidden by Company policy. Pressure suits, even the slatternly variety favored by the Company, cost money, don't you know. And what's more, decanting the remains of a picker who has turned prima ballerina and torn a hole in his suit the size of Lake Superior means paying the lucky decantor at least time and a half, if not double, and that is intolerable—so terpsichore, or any other form of low gravity acrobatics is strongly discouraged.

And there is another matter that makes it a challenge to work effectively in a pressure suit, and I think, seeing as I am in the middle of describing a daring rescue, this would be the perfect time to present it. It is a condition that for once is not the fault of the Moon's meager gravity, but instead the work of that far more treacherous hombre, the vacuum. You see, a pressure suit, when sealed up, filled with air, and introduced to the vacuum, promptly puffs up like a valedictorian on graduation day and takes on the appearance of a collection of fat sausages strung together in the shape of a man, or if you prefer, a particularly unsightly haggis, and thereafter cooperates with its wearer much as the haggis might in similar circumstances. If it were not for the accordion-fold pleats sewn into elbow, knee, hip, and shoulder joints, the occupant of the haggis would be unable to move his bloated limbs more than a few inches in any direction. So practicing terpsichore, trapeze, or three-card Monte on the Moon not only requires precise timing and an abundance of skill at being a low-flying projectile, but requires these while encased in an unwieldy haggis anxious to burst at the seams.

As we watched, the two men began to probe the dust for the sunken sled, using of all things our old friend the picker's "toothpick." Once they had sounded the sled sufficiently to determine its location and overall dimensions, the dust boat was maneuvered into position behind where the sled was buried. Then, with the dust boat in its new place, one man took a large roll or bundle from a locker on the parade float. While the first man held the bundle, the other took hold of a line attached to it and leapt over the sled, or its reputed resting place, and landed back aboard the Beast. As he flew over the dust, the bundle unrolled behind him, and suddenly a strange new object, an immense flattened gray doughnut at least six feet across, lay upon the dust, and immediately began to sink.

Finally, I couldn't stand it any more and said, "What in blazes do you suppose that is?" I did not expect an answer, but in this I was disappointed.

"It's the inside of a tire," Calvin answered, a bit too readily for my taste. "A big one too, like on the Beast. Many of your larger sorts of tire have an interior skin that can be inflated with air. Even some of the better steam buggies have them, I'm told."

"What do they want with that?" I wondered aloud.

Fortunately, Calvin had no ready answer for this, so we stared out the rear viewport and waited for the show, whatever it might be, to begin. Were they going to dive for supplies as we had done, or try to raise the sled itself from the dusty depths? I couldn't imagine how a doughnut, however oversized and underdone it might be, could help in this, but I was soon enlightened. One side of the doughnut, the side nearest the reputed location of the buried sled, sank rapidly, too rapidly if that is possible, into the dust. As it turned out, that side of the doughnut had lead weights attached, like the ones on a fishing line only bigger, and these sent the doughnut straight to the bottom. Each man, one on the digger and one in the dust boat, held the end of a line secured to the now sunken doughnut. Then the dust boat, piloted by the third man, sailed around to the side opposite to where the doughnut had disappeared. And with that change completed, the orientation of the lines also changed, so that one came out of the dust on the port side, held by the man on the digger, and the other emerged to starboard, and was held by the man on the dust boat. I don't think I comprehended it at the time, but the effect of the maneuver had been to draw the flattened doughnut under the sled. This is something like what is occasionally done in ocean-going ships when they spring a leak. A sail is passed beneath the hull to keep the water out, more or less. (This is done aboard sailing ships, of course, if it is done at all, for only they carry the canvas necessary to do it. I don't know what ocean-going steamships do in such circumstances, but I expect they operate like riverboats: once their hulls are stove in, and the dogs and gamblers have leapt over the side, they simply sink.)

As I should have guessed, the line leading to the dust boat was actually an air hose, and a cylinder of air was soon coupled to it. Nothing seemed to happen for a minute or so, then the dust above the sled began to stir, then flow away on all sides, like the water on top of a breaching whale, and after another minute we saw shapes emerge in the dust. They were familiar shapes, for the most part, and soon we were able to recognize certain items belonging to our lost cache of supplies. Before very much longer, the sled itself became visible, perching smugly on the upper surface of the mighty doughnut, which was now fully engorged with air and inflated to half the size of a house. I believe I said before that these fellows seemed far more prepared for our rescue than we were. After witnessing this feat, I was prepared to double and redouble that bid.

We watched in fascination as the man who had hopped to the risen sled tossed item after item of what were once our supplies to the man on the dust boat. Not a single one ended up in the dust. Then, when the sled was empty, the man on the dust boat crossed back over to the digger, and the two of them escorted the sled itself onto the parade float, which was now piled high with our goods. After adding in the two low-gravity acrobats, and the sled, there seemed to be precious little space left for us.

"Calvin," I said slowly, "I hate to even entertain such a thought about our three saviors over there, but do you think it's possible that rather than being rescued, we've just been robbed?"

"At this point I'm pretty certain that we're being robbed," he said. "Now the question is, will we be rescued into the bargain?"

"They were good enough to supply us with air and water. That must count for something," I offered.

"The water!" Bemis exclaimed. "Yes. Let's see if there's enough to rouse the Beast. I'll pour it down his gullet." And he did so, then he caressed a number of knobs and switches in order to direct the precious fluid through the machine's vitals.

Then I noticed that the dust boat was moving again. It soon left the digger and began to draw away.

"Calvin," I said quietly, "I was joking before, or at least half joking, but I think we have just been robbed, and left to fend for ourselves."

Bemis looked up from his gauges to witness the departure. We turned to look out the starboard viewport as the thieves moved past us, their bow wave sparkling, then turned to the forward port and watched as they sped away in front of us.

"We would have been better off with a canoe full of red Indians," I said. "They would have scalped us, sure, but not so completely."

Then as we watched, the dust boat loaded with our precious supplies, to say nothing of our precious salvation, began to turn, negotiating a broad glowing arc through the dust. After half a minute it was visible out the port side viewport, and was curving back in our direction.

"What are they doing?" Calvin said.

"Perhaps they've had a change of heart," I offered.

"I'll ask them," he said, reaching for the radio's controls. "Assuming they'll answer. I wouldn't if I were the thief."

"Wait," I said, "now it looks like they're traveling in circles." The dust boat had come about in a wide turn off our port bow, and was now steaming straight toward us. "They can't mean to ram us, can they?"

"What would be the point in that?" Bemis said. "It would simply wreck their boat. The Beast has a far tougher hide than they do."

But, although it was coming ever closer to the digger, the dust boat was still steering hard to port, and by the time it was back to within a half dozen yards of us, it had turned a full three hundred and sixty degrees, until at last it came to rest with its stern directly ahead of us, just a few yards beyond the digger's great claw. Then one of the acrobats leapt from the heavily laden parade float onto the claw itself and made fast a line to it.

"This is beginning to look like a rescue again," I said.

The man bounded back to the parade float, and to my immense satisfaction knocked a piece of booty into the dust as he landed. Those men were good, no doubt of that, good like a saint is good, but fortunately they were not perfect. (For my part, I am a skeptic when it comes to perfection. It is a fine thing to pursue, but, like great wealth or an unusually beautiful woman, may Heaven help you should you ever manage to catch it. Oh, it's fine for a time, perhaps even a long time, perhaps even a month, but then where do you go from there?) Plus the lost item had the look of vacuum jerky about it, so I was doubly pleased.

The radio crackled for a moment, then a new voice said, "Cap'n'll have the price a that jerky outta yer share, now won't he," and the voice laughed.

"He kin eat it then. I'd not have such vittles if I was adrift a month," claimed another voice. "I tell ya, shipmate, a man which—"

"Stow it, Chalk," said the voice of the pilot. "I need you men quiet now." Then, directing his transmission to us, he said, "So have you got the digger fired up then?"

"Fired up?" Bemis said, still staring out the forward port. He pulled his eyes away to inspect a cluster of gauges, whose needles, I noticed, were inching their way up their dials. "Uh, yes, nearly," he said, "but I doubt we'll move very much."

"That was a nice bit of piloting," I said to the radio.

"Thank'y," came the reply. "She's a worthy craft, the dust boat, but she turns slow, and won't back up for boogers, so it takes a bit a doin' to get her into position. Now, when I give the word, I want you to put that monster into gear and give it all the steam you've got. Can you do that?"

"Sure thing," Calvin said, and he glanced at the gauges again. Their needles were nearly vertical by then, and, although I knew little of gauges—I'm more of a wheel-and-rudder man when given my 'druthers —that seemed a good sign.

Over on the dust boat, one of the men reached out with the same six-foot toothpick he'd used to sound the sled, and batted aside a restraining hook holding the two sides of the dust boat's aluminum skin together at the stern. Apparently this was our cue. "A'right now," came the voice of our deliverer, "put 'er in gear and lay on the boogerin' steam."

We did as instructed. There was no response from the Beast for a moment, and the line holding us to the dust boat drew taut as the craft ahead of us started to move, then the steam took hold and we began to inch forward as well.

"We're moving, Cal!" I crowed. "By Heaven, we're moving."

It wasn't much of a speed, as yet, about the pace of a snail in top condition, but we were moving, and that qualified as a miracle in my religion, if only a miracle on the proportions of a snail. And soon we were picking up speed, to the breakneck pace of a man out for a stroll. He would have to be an old man, mind you, probably an octogenarian, and walking with a cane, but he could beat a snail, at least in the long haul, and that was enough. The reason we could travel even at that pace was because when the dust boat started moving forward, the two sides of its skin, now released, separated themselves and left a space that was relatively free of dust in which the digger could creep along. It was ingenious, although not without some precedent. Apparently certain waterfowl, geese for example, employ a similar principle when they fly in their characteristic V-shaped phalanx. The bird before blocks the wind, or a part of it, from the bird behind, and the dust boat was doing much the same thing for us.

We rode along in silence for a while then, thoroughly enjoying the fact that we were moving at all. By now we were roaring along at nearly the pace of a dog. Yes, you guessed it, an old dog, and one with three legs, but three good legs.

After a minute, I said, "Is it my imagination, or is the level of the dust dropping?"

Bemis looked out the starboard port, or maybe it was the other one. He stared at the dust for a while and eventually said, "I think you're right. Are we going out the way we came in, or another way?"

"I think we are into new territory," I said, "but I can't be certain. I don't suppose we have a compass?"

"No," he said.

"I imagine it's in the dust boat then," I said, and gestured vaguely out the front viewport.

Bemis gave me a withering look, and making little effort to hide his condescension, said, "The Moon has no magnetic field to speak of, Sam. Even if we had a compass it wouldn't do us a lick of good."

"Oh yes," I said quickly. "I know that." And I did, now that Bemis had told me.

"In any case, now that I think of it, the Beast never turned from his original course, so we must be heading for the other side of the crater," he concluded. And indeed we were. As the dust receded, the rim wall of Farley's Crater began to grow ahead of us, until it blotted out a significant portion of sky.

The damnable dust was at last behind us, and we followed the dust boat up an incline, which in turn put us onto a narrow road, this presumably leading either through, into, or over the rim wall. I was about to say that we had little choice in the matter, since we were still attached to our benefactors by a stout line, but of course the Beast could have parted that trifle with little more than a shrug. There seemed no point in such a reckless, not to say rude, course of action however, for they had all of our supplies on the parade float. We wouldn't have made it a mile before we would have to be rescued all over again. So we came over the rim wall together, and eventually arrived at what even a lime-hued neophyte such as myself could recognize as the entrance to a mine.

The first and most obvious signs of the mine were the mountains of tailings laid out all around it like the seven hills of Rome. I've just said they were mountains, and I admit this is an exaggeration, but a worthy one I think, since they were mighty tall for piles of tailings (which, by the way, are the dross cast aside after the valuable bits have been removed), and mighty steep by terrestrial standards, and thus inspired just a pinch of awe. Perhaps you have noticed on Earth how a pile of dirt or sand will slide down into a mound whose sides cannot get any steeper than a certain angle, no matter how you try to pile it higher. On the Moon, where the gravitational force is far less oppressive, more of a gentle tug at the coat tails than the usual kick in the pants, the piles of mine tailings we saw around us were far more precipitous than those back home. Given the right state of mind, such as might come from being spared a slow asphyxiation, they appeared almost comical, looking more like a collection of dunce caps than proper hills.

Beyond these, there was a small bay or inlet cut into the outer rim wall (for, if I have not made it clear, we were firmly on the outside of Farley's Crater by then), and just beyond that was the open maw of a mine.

Chapter Two

The dust boat, with the digger close behind, crawled around the mountains of tailings and onto a flattened area just outside the rough hole in the rim wall that was the entrance to the mine. This place was home to a collection of mining equipment and conveyances, including a partially disassembled traction engine, ore carts in various stages of repair, and even a fairly formidable digging leviathan. This object, though undoubtedly a fine machine, was not in a weight class equal to that of the Beast and was no threat to his hegemony, but it certainly could have fought on the undercard without disgrace.

The dust boat came to a stop on a spot crisscrossed with tire tracks that lay just beyond the entrance to the mine, and Bemis brought the digger to a halt directly behind it. The two machines extinguished their power plants then, and in the process released quantities of excess steam, which froze and fell to the ground in record time. Once the Beast was in repose, we reached for our helmets, eager to escape the confines of the digger's microscopic pilot house, despite having no idea of what might be ahead for us.

"You don't suppose they'll have water enough for a bath?" Bemis wondered aloud.

"A bath?" I said, fitting one of the cylinders of air we'd been given onto a bracket on the back of his pressure suit. "Well now, ain't you the nob." Then, recalling how long it had been since his last encounter with soap and water, and the exertions we had undertaken in the meantime, I modified my opinion. "I expect they'll have enough to spare once they've caught the scent of you."

"And I don't suppose you have an odor," he said.

"Not that I've noticed," I said, perhaps a bit disingenuously, but not entirely so. At that point I had been keeping company with my own odor for so long that it had finally tired of making my life, or at least my nose, miserable, and thrown in the sponge. Thereafter, like a picture hanging for years in the same location, or a debt owed to a man long in the grave, its presence went unnoticed. I don't know why this happens, but I consider it solid proof of the existence of a loving and merciful God. Bemis and I successfully negotiated the Dutch oven, then stood outside in the dim earthlight and watched with mixed emotions as the low gravity acrobats unshipped our former prospecting gear and performed a ruthless triage of it. Air cylinders, water, foodstuffs (including the loathsome vacuum treated varieties), and perennials such as the pick and shovel were placed back aboard the sled they had started on, and everything else, objects we had paid dearly if discursively to possess, was pitched unceremoniously onto the tailings. I was nearly moved to lend a hand in this operation, just to bid farewell to goods I had cherished in simpler times, but then they got to tossing around the explosives and I decided I was moved near enough as it was and left them to their work. In fact they were quite solicitous of the explosives and provided them with a choice berth aboard the sled. Then the third man from the dust boat, its pilot, beckoned to us with a wave of his gloved hand, so we turned away from the disposition of our possessions, and followed him into the black mouth of the mine.

There were no electric lights decorating the tunnel that stretched away into the rock, and naturally there were no torches or other forms of oxygen-fueled lighting either. I reached for the switch on my helmet that activated its headlamp, but by then the battery that powered it was so depleted that its light would have failed to illuminate the inside of a walnut. Bemis tried his, and the result was much the same. Fortunately, our guide had a battery for his lamp that had been recently fed, and it lit the way just fine for him, so all we had to do was follow along and not let him and his beacon get too far ahead.

By the light left in our benefactor's wake, we could see that the steep, descending tunnel was occasionally shored up with posts and plates of steel or aluminum wedged or pounded into the rock. Those occasions were few, however, and substantially far apart, like Thanksgiving, Groundhog Day, and the Fourth of July, and were just as eagerly anticipated. To me it seemed a meager collection, considering the countless tons of rock poised to come down on us. But the Moon is forgiving in this department, if in little else, due to the lax gravitation once again, and it turned out that the rare occasions these miners had chosen to celebrate with shoring were enough to keep the roof over our heads where it belonged.

After perhaps a hundred yards of burrowing down into the crater's rim, the tunnel leveled off and expanded into a cavern, and there a succession of ore carts rested, partially filled with rock. Two men in pressure suits, their helmet lamps robustly ablaze, shoveled ice ore, or mine tailings, or perhaps peppermint candy—I couldn't have told one from the other at that point in my career, and I'm fond of peppermint candy—from a long pile on one side of the cavern into the carts. I could see immediately why they had coveted our shovel.

We wormed past the men doing the shoveling and came to a stop before a big sheet of aluminum that after a moment I perceived to be an airlock. We passed into it and out the other side all together, as it was considerably more spacious than the Beast's Dutch oven, and on its far side we were able to escape our pressure suits for the first time in a decade, or so it seemed. We had not withdrawn ourselves from their company in the digger's cabin, even though they had overstayed their welcome, because trying to put them on in there had made the difficulty plenty clear. Once emptied of their contents, our suits, minus their helmets, were taken up by two of the four men in the chamber beyond the airlock, thrown into that same airlock, and straightaway subjected to the rigors of the vacuum.

Bemis and I must have appeared puzzled—I wrongly assumed that our pressure suits were to be deeded to the mine owners along with our other goods, and hoped vaguely that they would survive the triage—because one of the men said, "A few minutes in the vacuum kills the fleas, as well as a good portion of the bacteria." His tone was only moderately condescending, which as a professional greenhorn I appreciated, but I had no idea what a bacterium was at the time, or in truth even today, as I can only judge by the claims of the scientists who lobby for their existence, and scientists are in the business of inventing impossibilities. Still, if these bacteria kept company with fleas, I reckoned they were getting what they deserved.

The man, who was tall and thin with a face and manner located somewhere between those of a parson and an undertaker, said, "Welcome aboard the Deirdre, gentlemen, although I suppose your gentility remains to be seen. I am first mate Lang. You may call me Mister Lang, First Mate, or sir, whichever you prefer." He was dressed in the standard issue uniform of the Moon, flannel shirt and bib overalls, but it was the cleanest and best preserved such uniform I had ever seen, outside of those still supine upon a shelf in a dry goods store.

"I'm Sam Clemens," I said. "Of the Missouri Clemenses," I added, trusting that my family's reputation had not reached the Montes Caucasus ahead of me, "and this is my partner Calvin Bemis. And you can call us Sam and Calvin, I suppose." I offered my hand at this point, but it was left alone on the field and eventually was obliged to retire.

"You look in better shape than some we've seen," said Lang. "Garrett and Watkins were three-quarters in the grave by the time we got them aboard—but we'll send you down to Mister Kent for a good going-over to satisfy the formalities, and chase down any remaining fleas." I tried to look indignant over this, but was betrayed by the untimely need for a scratch. "He'll see to it that you get cleaned up." And here he wrinkled his nose just a bit. I too detected an odor, which I assumed was due to Bemis, but in fact the scent I was imbibing was a permanent resident of the Deirdre mine. In another week I would fail to notice it at all.

I said, "So are you the foreman here?"

"Like I told you—Clemens is it—I'm first mate of the Deirdre." I had known first mates aplenty in the piloting trade, but the profession felt out of place inside the Moon. Still, most of them were kin enough to a foreman to fill the bill, so I let it rest. I had also determined by some process of elimination that it was the mine itself that they called the Deirdre, and so I was content. "Don't fret, Clemens," the first mate continued, "Mister Kent will see that you're fed and watered when he's done with you." My ears pricked up like a coyote's upon discovering a prairie dog. I'd thought I was content, but had failed to consult with my stomach in the matter, and any news of food was now profoundly interesting to me. I could not recall the last time I had eaten, let alone eaten well, and was reluctant to do so, for I feared that if I did and remembered the full pleasure of it, I might descend into a bottomless melancholy, since chances were excellent that I would never experience its like again.

"Thank you, um, Mister Lang. And thank you in particular for our rescue. We owe you a great debt of —"

"Yes, yes," he said, "the captain will go over all that soon enough." He turned to one of the men standing behind him. "Perkins, see that these men get to Mister Kent without delay."

The man named Perkins glanced at us and said, "Aye, Mister Lang."

Then Lang turned to the other men and said, "And you. Think you'd never seen a man pulled out of the dust before. Find yourselves some work to do in a hurry, else I'll find it for you," and the men scurried away into a selection of tunnels like their backsides were on fire.

The man Perkins turned abruptly and led us away down a tunnel. This passage through the rock was as straight as a corkscrew, as roomy as a prairie dog's hole—if he hasn't eaten lately—and rose and fell like the stock exchange at the Apocalypse, and yet it proved to be one of the better tunnels they had in the Deirdre, because it was decorated with the occasional —the very occasional—incandescent bulb, and was full of that most necessary of substances: air.

As it turned out, many of the tunnels thereabouts were not so fortunate and, although fully as dark, snug, and convoluted, lacked this all-important feature, and thus had to be navigated in a pressure suit. I will have more to say on these later. Much more.

We kept pace with Perkins, and were soon decanted into another chamber furnished with, if you can credit it, two electric lights, and both of them operating at the same time. I decided that its owner must be a considerable potentate in these parts. The chamber also had a smell about it that sent a thrill of anticipation through my vitals, and a corresponding torrent of saliva into my mouth. There was food here, said my nose, real food. Not greasy sludge squeezed out of a package or meat destroyed by vacuum, not even otherwise respectable produce imprisoned in a metal can, but real food. Hot food. Food treated like a Christian and cooked in a pot.

"Mister Kent," said Perkins, "here're the men we fished out of the soup. They're likely not worth the air they breathe, but they aren't dead as yet, and came with a decent haul of goods to add to stores." It came to me as Perkins was speaking that his was a voice I recognized, and suddenly I understood that this man Perkins, whom I had mistaken for a mere mortal, was in fact our chief savior, the pilot of the dust boat.

I turned, and before he could refuse my ministrations, grasped his hand in mine and said, "I believe I have been remiss, sir, for I realize now that it is you who I need to thank in particular for our deliverance."

"Thank you, Mister Perkins," said the man Kent, ignoring my attempt at idolatry.

Perkins said, without much english on it, "You're welcome, mate. I've seen worse fools, I expect." This amounted to high praise from Perkins, but I didn't understand this at the time, and accepted the remark at its face value. He was unimpressed by idolatry, however, or at least my efforts in that line, and left us to Mister Kent without another word.

Once we had lost Perkins, Kent took charge, and right away he began to peer at us with a prejudiced eye and poke his fingers into our tender parts like we were two carcasses of mutton, and questionable mutton at that. He even insisted that we open our mouths to him and extend our tongues. If he had been introduced by Perkins as the mine's resident physician I would have been mollified, if not entirely reassured, but this information had been missing from our savior's brief catechism, and the powerful smell of roasting flesh on the air caused my thoughts to turn in darker directions. Mind you, I did not think for a minute that these men tucked into long pig at their suppers, but I thought it for a part of that time, and that was long enough.

As it turned out, Mister Kent was both resident physician and *chef de cuisine*, all wrapped up in one small, round, strikingly hirsute package. I say he was strikingly hirsute, even in that kingdom of the hirsute sex that is the Moon, because he came attached to a voluminous and fiery red beard, which was a great novelty there, and advertised in its luxuriance that its owner did not venture out of doors much, at least as it is done on the Moon. This is because nothing in the world is more troublesome in a pressure suit's helmet than a bumper crop of facial hair. There is nothing wrong, in most cases, with a mustache, or even a moderate, restrained spread of beard, but a massive growth like Mister Kent's can accomplish an astonishing variety of mischief within the confines of a pressure helmet—astonishingly lethal, more often than not. Try catching a selection of your whiskers in the seal between helmet and neck ring, and it will likely be the last thing you do. The pain you experience when you work to pull them free, without the use of your hands mind you, is enough to make you wish you were dead. Fortunately, because of the faulty seal, you will die of asphyxiation or decompression before the pain gets that severe. However, I feel it necessary to point out that this in no way exonerates the hat. It is still public enemy number one as regards articles of apparel on the Moon. There is not a hair's breadth of competition in it, and I assert that a man who goes about in the Moon sporting an extensive batch of facial hair and wearing a hat is a man who either never goes onto the surface at all, or is destined to do so only once.

Despite the cooking food, it was cold in that cavern, as it generally was everywhere in the Deirdre (and everywhere on the Moon, except where it is blazing hot), and I found I missed my shirt and overalls. My under-drawers, though comprehensive, were inadequate to the conditions, and were drafty in any case, due to the many worn patches and downright holes they had collected in our travels together. So when Kent, whether in his capacity as physician or as chef I could not say, required us to abandon even this last shred of clothing, I was not pleased. But all was forgiven once he handed us a sponge, a sliver of soap, and a pail full of water—and not just any water, but hot water, or at least water tolerably warm to the touch. This, although not quite the copiously liquid affair one is likely to get back home, was the bath Bemis had longed for (and that I had longed to see him receive), and despite the short measure of water involved, it was glorious, because the water was not only delightfully wet, but deliciously warm as well.

Mister Kent went away under one of the electric lights, presumably to attend to food, and left us to our ablutions. Then when we were about finished, and the water in the pail had turned a deep mahogany in appreciation, a new man appeared and offered us each a set of under-drawers, stylish red ones, followed by a shirt and overalls. None of these garments were new, or even particularly youthful, and they had the scars to prove it, but they were clean, and in that moment that was everything.

As I got inside those clothes and Bemis did the same, I said, "Hot water, clean clothes, and if I am not mistaken, real proper cooked food to come. Perhaps we have died and gone to heaven after all."

Calvin smiled. "Well, a second-hand heaven at any rate."

"Second-hand?" I scoffed. "Some parishioners are never satisfied. Next you'll be telling me you want a shave."

In fact we got a shave (or two of them, one apiece, as is customary), but not right then. We were offered the opportunity prior to our meeting with the captain, and we accepted eagerly. But it was a waste of the lather in my opinion, because by the time he was finished with us, the captain had sheared us so close he nearly drew blood.

After dressing, we were let loose into the general population for mess call. I'm sure the hall was enchanting, and the company of quality no doubt, and entertaining, but all Bemis and I could notice for a good while was the food, which was suitably magnificent. There were three courses, if you can believe it. At the feast's heart was a noble stew of pork—at least I think it was pork—but whichever of God's creatures it was made from, it wasn't rotten, or vacuum desiccated, and in addition contained part of an onion, and what I suspect was a carrot, or something that could pass for a carrot if the light wasn't good, which it wasn't. And to accompany the stew there was bread. The loaf it sprung from was as old as Methuselah and as impenetrable as the Mormon bible, but it was bread nonetheless. The astute reader will object that this is only two courses, and even then considerable leeway must be granted to the bread. But the third course was perhaps the best of all. Each man, not just we who had been left for dead in Farley's Crater, but all eight men present, whether deserving or not, was given a measure of whiskey, and not just any old whiskey, but bourbon whiskey, if memory serves.

In addition to the three course meal, a quart of water was provided to each man: water fresh from the resonance engine, and thus as pure and untainted by sin or the presence of bacteria as the heart of a saint—not that that increased its appeal to me, who had grown up drinking, if that is the right term, the rich red-brown soup ladled out of the Mississippi river. As I have discussed elsewhere, a quart of Mississippi water has so much of the Earth in it that it eats like a meal, and can best be enjoyed with a spoon.

After supper we were offered the aforementioned shave, or the means for accomplishing it, and after the operation was finished, taken to see the captain. We were not told the purpose of the audience, and assumed it to be social in nature. This turned out not to be the case.

The captain of the Deirdre (for this was how he styled himself and no one appeared to question it) had a berth to himself, as his station deserved. That is to say, he occupied a small cavern, or large depression in the rock, that was entirely his own, with the luxury of a door, fashioned from a sheet of aluminum of course, and an electric light. He only had one such, however, while the estimable Mister Kent had possessed a matched pair. Then again, Kent was lord of a vast domain comprising both kitchen and sickbay, to say nothing of the chicken coop, while the captain's cabin held little more than a desk and a bunk, plus a sizable collection of rocks.

Captain Eustace Merriwether did not rise from his chair to greet us when we were shown inside. At first he didn't even look up from the nest of books and papers on his desk. It was a real desk by the way, not a sheet of aluminum—by which I mean that it was made of wood, presumably by someone on Earth who had made intimate acquaintance with a tree. This was a thing rarer to see than fresh air on the Moon, but the captain of the Deirdre had obtained it somehow. There were two chairs in the little cabin, which were in reality spent aluminum hogsheads. Calvin and I planted our backsides in them without permission and waited with a patience only available to the well-fed until Captain Merriwether deigned to look up, which eventually he did.

"Welcome aboard the Deirdre, gentlemen. I assume you are well, or well enough, and that Mister Kent has seen to your immediate needs."

"Yes, thank you," I said. "Everyone has been most kind."

"And generous," put in Bemis, as unaware of the true nature of the thing as a dog at Sunday school, or myself for that matter. But our enlightenment was in the offing, and gaining on us like a lee shore.

Captain Merriwether picked up a thin ledger, glanced briefly at it, then returned his gaze to us, saying, "Very well. Now, can you men read, and do sums to any degree?"

"Certainly," I said. "Some people are even persuaded that I can write as well," I added. "They are credulous people, for the most part, but—"

"Good," the captain interrupted. "This is an account of your debits and credits as of this moment." He held up the opened ledger, then passed it to me. "Please be so good as to satisfy yourselves that it is accurate and complete."

I took the book and began to look it over. Calvin leaned out of his hogshead to peer at it too. In it, each moment of our long day of deliverance was chronicled, and a price tag attached.

"Do you mean to say," I said, looking up from the carnage, "that we are expected to pay for our rescue?"

Merriwether said, "The Deirdre is not a charity, Mister Clemens."

"Judging by these figures, that is abundantly clear," I said. I took a moment to recover from the initial shock of it, then interrogated the ledger more closely. "I remember the air cylinders and the carboy of water, but what is this about six articles from the 'slops chest'?"

"You're wearing them, sir, or half of them. Mister Bemis wears the other half." Any normal man, even a lawyer, would have smiled upon saying this, but Merriwether just sat there impassively, stroking the gray-brown stubble on his face that would any day now declare itself a beard.

I looked down at the worn and tattered overalls I was dressed in. "Why, I could have bought a new suit of clothes in St. Louis for this price, good clothes too, or a full set of boot laces in New York."

"You're a long way from St. Louis," said Merriwether. There was no denying that.

"Sam," said Calvin, pointing at the far page, "they've charged us for the bath, thin as it was, and for the shave, which we did for ourselves."

"With the Deirdre's razor, soap, and water," said the captain.

"And then there's the price of the rescuing itself." Bemis pointed again.

"I could buy a horse for that," I insisted. "Maybe even a genuine Mexican plug."

The captain shook his head. "You couldn't buy a horse for a thousand dollars on the Moon, as I'm sure you're aware. My men are highly skilled at what they do. Surely you don't expect them to save your lives for nothing."

"But our supplies," Bemis said. "Surely they are worth something. They cost us enough."

"You have been duly credited for those. What we have use for anyhow." The Deirdre's captain favored us with a sharp gaze. "By what Mister Perkins tells me, the two of you would have been asphyxiated in another few hours. Are your lives not worth the price of, what did you call it, Clemens, a Mexican plug?"

Calvin looked at me and said, "I hate to admit it, but he's right, Sam."

"Yes," I admitted, "I suppose he is, but I could have done without a shave if I'd known it was going to cost me two dollars." I sighed, then said, "Very well, sir. I can see which side the bread is buttered on now that it's fallen in my lap, and, I am grateful for our deliverance, and the meal, and for Calvin's bath too, despite the price. So, if you will be good enough to pass me your pen and a scrap of paper, I'll write out a marker for the full amount."

"And how long will I be holding that marker, sir? Until you and your partner strike it rich, I suppose."

"Exactly," I said.

Captain Merriwether would no doubt have laughed at this point, if he were at all disposed toward laughter, which he was not. Instead he said, "Come, gentlemen. Have you no money at all? I am not a difficult man. I will gladly accept gold, silver, air, ice, foodstuffs, even tradable goods. Have you nothing of value?" He knew perfectly well that we did not, but his offer to accept payment in anything from Fabergé eggs to chicken's eggs was part of the play, and he didn't want to short the second act.

"I believe we have a dollar," I said, with as much pride as I could muster. This was not a hundredth, perhaps not a thousandth, part of what was needed, but with a dollar between us we were not vagrants, not entirely.

"Yes," said Bemis. "It's in the digger. Stuck into the instructions manual for safe keeping, I believe."

Calvin looked at me then, and I immediately understood what his hopeful, forlorn stare presaged.

"Are you sure?" I ventured.

He said, "What choice do we have, Sam?"

"Well now," I began, working up my best drummer's pitch. "There is the digger. It's worth quite a bit more than what we owe of course. Worth quite a lot in fact, if valued correctly. It's an absolutely first rate machine." I felt somewhat as if I were negotiating the sale of my mother, so naturally I was determined that she fetch a good price. "However, I expect we can work out something, perhaps a portfolio of shares, to compensate us for the overage."

The captain was shaking his head, and no doubt would have smiled ruefully, if he were ever disposed to smile. "We have no use for a digger in the Deirdre, gentlemen."

"Oh, yes," I said, undaunted, "I saw on the way in that you already have a digger in stock, but it can't hold a candle to the Beast, and that's a fact. Why, he can—"

"We have no use for a digger, Clemens. That thing you saw on the surface came with Garrett and Watkins and is only good for towing ore cars to the pulverizing mill."

"But you can't do a thing in the mining line without a digger," Bemis insisted.

If Merriwether had been capable of laughter this surely would have been his moment, but instead he said, "Who told you that?"

Neither Bemis nor I had much to say about this, because our authority on the subject was none other than the man who'd sold it to us, and even we could see the hole in that argument. If you cared to, you could throw a cow through it, in the dark. "Why, it's common knowledge," I said desperately.

"It's bunk," Merriwether said. This turned out to be a good description for most everything we knew, but we didn't know even that much at the time. "Take a look around you," he continued. I successfully resisted the urge to inspect my surroundings. "That digger of yours is well over a dozen feet tall and more than half of that across the beam. You might as well dig out a gopher's hole with an elephant. No, a big machine like that is useless once you've dug out quarters, and perhaps the initial shaft." He frowned. "No. I'm mighty sorry, boys, but we've got no use for it. No use at all."

We sat in silence for a while, then at last Calvin said, "So what are we to do then?" In fact he should have seen the answer coming a mile away, but alas it was over his horizon.

"You'll work it off, like Garrett and Watkins, and some others in the crew. You're hardly the first men we've pulled out of the dust." As it happened, the rescue of miners from Farley's Crater was a going concern in the Deirdre. If we'd been paying attention, the presence of the dust boat and the efficiency of its operation might have told us that.

"And how long is that likely to take?" I asked. "You see, we're anxious to get to prospecting as soon as possible."

"Not so long," he said. "You lay off the luxuries like whiskey and soap and water, it shouldn't take you more than a year or two, three at the outside." And if I didn't know better, I would have sworn that Captain Merriwether smiled, but I think it was just a trick of the light from the incandescent bulb.

Chapter Three

And so we began our term of indentured servitude in the Deirdre mine. In retrospect—that distant height from which the road of one's life looks less rutted, and the muddy patches not so deep—it seems that we were fortunate in our servitude, at least for a while. As the perspicacious reader may have noticed, there was a lot Bemis and I didn't know about the mining trade, in fact it would have taken a thorough search of the territory to find something about it that we did know. When it came to the gritty details of extracting the riches of the Moon, rumor, wild fantasy, and a selection of harebrained schemes was about all we had in stock, and thus our time served in the Deirdre taught us a great deal. The lessons did not always come easily, more of the opposite in fact, but in the end we got our money's worth, even if we didn't know it at the time.

In honor of our ignorance, we were assigned a task that I thought more suited to a mule than a pair of men in pressure suits. All work of any significance in the Deirdre, except that of Mister Kent and Mister Lovelace, who was master of the mine's resonance engine, was done in the vacuum, and there was no pressure gear on hand that would suit a mule, or any mule available to object to it, so Bemis and I were elected. The job consisted in hauling hods full of ice, metal ore, or tailings out of the various tunnels where they had been discovered and up to a depot where the goods could be further inspected, consolidated, then shoveled into a series of ore carts. These were then hauled up to the surface—by the power of a traction engine, when it was operational, or by the power of the men who had loaded them when it wasn't, which we soon learned was most of the time. It is a measure of the unpleasantness of the hod work that loading, and even propelling, the two-ton ore carts was considered better work than hod carrying—more of a job for a horse or an Irishman than a mule. The Deirdre had a fully functional traction engine which could have been used: it was at the heart of the dust boat. And it is a measure of the importance they assigned to the rescue (or capture, depending upon your point of view) of future hod carriers and ore cart wranglers that they did not for a moment consider dismantling the dust boat in order to use its traction engine to haul out ore.

Our work began deep in the mine, although not in its profoundest depths—we were too green as yet to plumb that netherworld—at a wide place in a pitch-dark tunnel where rock, ore, or some other material had been dug out. While we removed this material to the upper realms, we inspected it eagerly, hoping to distinguish the several species involved, namely ice, metal ores, and tailings—so already we were learning.

We were not responsible for definitively identifying any of these, indeed as "baby miners" we were discouraged from doing so, but the estimable Perkins, who was in charge of our instruction, was kind enough to present examples of each, so that we might not confuse them in the performance of our duty and eat into the profits of the mine.

The ice ore looked like vaguely lustrous black or gray lumps, sometimes as big as a man's head, and often shot through with blots and streaks of white. I had expected ice ore to be white, or perhaps green, and some of the best pieces were indeed nearly white, but most were shot through with dust and other impurities, and that made them harder to distinguish from the ordinary rock. Ice ore was a fairly regular, and welcome, passenger in our hod. The iron ore (for it was usually iron, not gold, silver, or even lead, alas) was generally darker, harder, and sometimes streaked with color, and was a less frequent traveler in the hod. The tailings consisted of dust, gravel, and a great many pieces of brownish-gray rock with nothing in particular to recommend them. This useless material was disappointingly ubiquitous, and there was always plenty of it available to fill up our hod. Forever on the lookout for a way to improve the quality, and reduce the effort, of my work, I asked Perkins why they didn't leave the tailings where they had started instead of hauling it all to the surface for deposition onto the seven hills.

"Inside of a week, all the tunnels would be choked with the stuff," he said through his suit's radio, as he instructed us in how to load the hod: large rocks on the bottom, not too full, but not too light, and try to transport only one species of material at a time, so as not to undo the careful triage our more skilled colleagues had performed.

"Why not dig out a place beside the tunnel to dump it in?" I instructed.

Perkins chuckled, and the beam of his lamp swept side to side as he shook his head. "And where would you put the tailings from that, ya silly booger?" he said. "You just tote your hod and leave the thinking to me and the captain." I offered that a mine that came with more ore in it and a good deal less tailings was the obvious solution, but Perkins was not amused, so I picked up the front end of the hod and we started up the tunnel.

There was more to this simple work than met the eye, and none of it in the procedure's favor. Then again, very little met the eye in that dungeon, unless it was formally introduced while one's headlamp was satisfactorily charged. It was a question, for instance, whether the job was worse going up or coming down. Each leg of the journey had its partisans, but I had trouble making up my mind, even after weeks of intensive study. Heading up-tunnel required a deal of heavy lifting, an entertainment to which I have never been much devoted. Plus, if one failed in his duty while manning the rearward position, even for an instant, he caused ore (or more likely tailings) to rain onto his helmet; while if one was in the van and lost his grip, the hod would capsize and loose its entire contents onto the man behind. Needless to say, I preferred the van when I could get it.

The down-tunnel leg might seem the nicer work, but it had its pitfalls as well. The tunnels were generally steep and occasionally precipitous, which was bad enough on the up leg, during which the lead man often had to climb while holding the handles of the hod behind him at the level of his boots, and the man behind had to hold his end over his head, if the roof would permit it. But things were arguably worse going down, despite an empty hod, because stumbling over a precipice and rolling on down the tunnel until stopped by something very hard was a regular feature of the trip. And so was losing one's way. This, like much that takes place on the Moon, is actually worse than it sounds.

You see, the tunnels split off from one another as they penetrate downhill into the rim, because digging, or blasting, a new tunnel was the way to find more ice. This is good news for the man headed out, as he could simply keep going uphill and trust that the tunnels would tend to unite and reduce his chances of making a wrong turn. But going downhill produced the opposite effect, as each new bifurcation provided a fresh opportunity to go wrong and end up lost in the depths.

And as I've said, this can be, and often is, worse than it sounds, for being lost in an overgrown rabbit warren inside the Moon is not the pleasant adventure that being lost in the woods, or the Gobi desert, is back home. In the Gobi desert, one cannot run out of air. Water maybe, but not air. Even spelunking the Carlsbad caverns will not deprive you of air—but the Moon will do it gladly given half a chance. On Earth, not even the dead of night will deprive you entirely of light. There are always the stars, or if those should fail, you can strike a match and take your bearings— but let your lamp battery expire under the Moon, and you will see nothing, no matter how long you may wait for your eyes to adapt. Nor can you strike a match, as you could in the Carlsbad caverns, because there is no air to support its combustion.

But surely, you say, one can call for help—but in this you would be mistaken, because the radio in your pressure suit, despite its best intentions, cannot communicate through solid rock. I could talk to Bemis, if we managed to get lost while lugging the same hod, but everyone else in the Deirdre was as beyond hearing as a man in the grave. Or nearly so. If one left his suit radio active, ghostly echoes and strange snatches of conversation could sometimes be heard, and if one found himself in one of the rare straight stretches of tunnel, he could hear transmissions from the far end preternaturally well—but things like that never happened when you were lost.

I know all this not from the tales of others, but because I experienced it myself, and more than once. Not the ultimate calamity of running out of air, fortunately—I passed on that—but I bought the rest of the package time and again.

Oddly enough, the first thing you do, or should do, upon deciding that you have got lost (invariably through taking a wrong fork on a downward run), is to extinguish your helmet lamp. One may indulge in a round of cursing either before or after this step, but it's best to keep it concise, for you may wish you had the air back in an hour or so. You want to think about conserving what light you have left, to say nothing of your air, and you want to do it while there's something left of it to conserve. Although it is arduous, and frightening, to make your way in total darkness, it is, for once, less difficult than it might sound, assuming that you know which way is up. If you do, it is just a matter of groping along the tunnel you have chosen to get lost in, crawling on hands and knees when in doubt about the footing, and each of you keeping a glove against one wall of the passage, which is never out of reach when it is there at all. When a tunnel's wall suddenly disappears, it is cause for celebration, and the lighting of a helmet lamp, for a gap in the wall signals the meeting of two tunnels, or their parting, if you were headed down, and is an opportunity to locate yourself, and an opportunity for disappointment.

The Deirdre's miners, having lost themselves often enough in the past, had scratched signs on the walls at a good many junctions to aid in navigation. So, if you encountered a gap in the walls, you turned on a lamp and peered around, looking, as the saying goes, for a sign. If one was present, and one or the other of you could puzzle out the meaning of a message along the lines of "B6+2" to any good effect, you then knew where you were. If not, or if there was no sign to be found, then the disappointment came, and after a round of oaths, the lamp would get extinguished and on you would go as before, until the next gap in the walls appeared. Oh, and don't leave the hod behind where you can't find it again, or the first mate will dock your share in the profits and you will see another week or two added to your sentence to cover the loss. Don't leave your hod partner behind either, even if you don't care for him overly much, as recollection of his abandonment will haunt you in later years, if his ghost doesn't get the job done first.

There was legend surrounding this brand of mishap, and as Calvin and I made up the latest batch of indentured greenhorns, we were deemed ripe for the telling of it. As with most such stories, it was likely apocryphal, but no less entertaining, and disturbing, for that. The tale was offered to us late one evening, or so claimed the holy clock in the engineering cave, whose pendulum had been precisely truncated so it could tell proper time (that is, Earth time) in the Moon. We lounged beneath the dim electric bulb in the steamy, sweltering comfort of the communal bed chamber—which, when the hammocks were stowed and a sheet metal table installed, was also the mess hall, as well as saloon and gambling den when Mister Lang was not around. The tale was told, with much encouragement and occasional embellishments from his mates, by a fellow named Gottschalk. He was one of the oldest, and by that I mean longest interred, crewmen of the Deirdre, a man who had chosen to follow Captain Merriwether, Lang, and Perkins into outer space to plunder the bowels of the Moon rather than continue in the dying whaling trade. (Whale oil is a drug on the market in the age of the resonance engine.) Gottschalk, whom the men called Chalk, had a substantial and livid collection of tattoos decorating his hide, which advertised, falsely now, his lost profession. These gave his weathered countenance a ghoulish aspect in the jaundiced light, which only served to enhance the impact of his tale.

"Not everyone's so lucky as you two pups," he began. We were briefly notorious for losing ourselves, then reappearing on our own steam, with less than an hour of air and even less battery life remaining to us. "More'n one man has come ta grief carryin' hod, and that's a fact. But they's one such I recall that was remarkable, and is a mystery to this day." He looked around at his mates, eyes shining. "You've heard tell a the man, I 'spect, even if he was a'fore yer time. Do ya recollect his name, shipmates?" (This is known on the lecture circuit as *ginning up the crowd.*)

"Perkins," said a wag. It goes without saying, I suppose, that Perkins was not present.

"No," piped up another. "It's Lang I'd not mind seein' lost. Leastwise for a week or so." Mister Lang was absent as well, and good-humored laughter followed. Lang, although a bit of a hard horse, was not truly disliked by the men, but the formalities must be observed in these matters or discipline will soon disintegrate.

"Naw," said Chalk. "As you well know, his name were Jones, John Jones, but fer the sake a the tellin' we'll call him jonah, for that's what he was, shipmates, sure's yer born."

This is a handle freighted with great significance in the sailing trade, and I knew, even if Chalk hadn't made it clear, that jonah was not so much the poor fellow's name as it was his occupation, at least in the Deirdre. You see, a jonah, if by some chance you do not know it, is a jinx, or more accurately, a man whom the rest of the crew believes to be a jinx, and once a soul is labeled thus, his life becomes a misery of distrust and isolation, or worse. In my experience, which is admittedly slim in this line, the jonah has rarely performed any specific act to earn his ignominy, although some such act may be alleged. Typically he finds the reputation accreting to him like barnacles attaching themselves to a ship's hull, and once it has stuck, it is just as hard to remove.

"So Jones was assigned to carry hod, as despite bein' a jonah he were still pretty raw." Chalk glanced at Bemis and me. "Now as you well know, totin' ore up-tunnel is a two man job, an' when Jones was on hod duty the man on the other end of the sticks nearly always come ta grief, by an' large." He glanced again at the two of us. "That means one way or t'other. The two a them would lose their way and nearly suffocate." Calvin and I looked at each other then, trying to calculate who would dare call the other jonah first and beat the rush. "Or the other man would put a boot wrong and pitch down a shaft, or tear open his suit on a outcropping an' lose a leg to the vacuum, or else come down with scurvy, the bloody flux, or the gripin' gut." All ills, no matter how incidental, are the jonah's fault, you see, especially, but not exclusively, if he is detected anywhere within a few hundred miles of the calamity. "Nothin' would happen ta Jones," Chalk continued, "'cept the gettin' lost, a course, but always to his shipmates, this bein' one of the ways a jonah is discovered ta begin with."

The men around me made noises of agreement, as the rules governing such travesties of justice were understood by all. I considered briefly whether I should contrive to sustain an injury, and thus insure myself against jonah-hood, but I decided to bide my time and purchase the policy only if the calamity looked imminent, as the premium was costly.

"As ya might figger," continued Chalk, "it soon was thought a trial ta be assigned ta haul ore with the man, and men were known ta cause their own selves a injury just ta duck the duty, and this only added to his evil reputation, don'tcha see." My sympathies had migrated considerably since the start of the tale, and were now firmly with the hapless John Jones. "Still, jonah or no, there needs ta be a man on the other end of the hod, so somebody was always coming down with the croup or bustin' a hose on his gear, always somethin', one way or t'other. One day a man named Murphy, who was a Irishman I believe, was aft of the hod, with Jones in front an' spangin' rocks offen Murphy's helmet fer his trouble no doubt, an' natur'ly, Jones being what he was, they got themselves lost, down in old D2 that was mostly played out even then. So Jones an' poor Murphy takes off down a false spur, as a jonah will do, and was lost. Anyhow, they didn't come back in a time Mister Perkins thought fit, an' word went out that they was likely to be lost. The men figgered there were no great harm in losing Jones, and some dared say we was all the better for it, but the man Murphy was well liked. Carried an honest hod, he did, an' could sing them moldy Irish ditties so's Mister Lang hisself would find a tear in his eye.

"Well, me and another man—" another man who was conveniently absent, and thus unavailable to corroborate the tale, I noted, "—we was sent down ta see if we could fetch 'em a'fore their air gave out. This was afore we'd marked the junctions proper, ya understand."

Bemis and I had tried to use some of these markings in our recent adventure, and had struggled to interpret them correctly. In the end we had survived through the intervention of a higher power, namely, dumb luck.

"Trouble was," continued Chalk, "they was blastin' a new hole at the end a D3, on account a the cap'n likin' the look a some rock from a outcropping down there which he reckoned might hold some heavy metals. We, the other man an' myself sent down ta D2, was somewhat vexed by this, as blastin' can knock loose a deal a rock even a fair distance away. A man was sent to tell Lang and his party they was supposed to lay off on the detonations for a spell, 'til Murphy and Jones was recovered, or gave up for dead, but there bein' a jonah aboard, the man took a wrong fork hisself an' ended up in D1, where they wasn't a soul, for it was played out.

"Anyways, we was down a fair piece into D2 and lookin' into the side spurs if they seemed like they mighta been tread in, but not goin' too far along any particular one, if ya get my meanin', when we hears a commotion over the radio, which we has kept on for just such a purpose, an' we knows we must be near ta them lost sheep, since everywhere else around us was solid rock 'cept straight on ahead. Well, we follows the tunnel 'til a light comes in view. We has our lamps shut down a course, so's we c'n see if anyone's there. It's dyin' out fast, that lamp, ya can practically see it goin', but it shows us Murphy and the jonah, and while their light is fadin' an' the last a their air wastin' away, they're a fightin' each other, arguin' over which way they oughta go. Natur'ly Jones wants to take 'em the wrong way. They sees us a comin' about then, an' they stops their bickerin' and starts running up-tunnel in our direction, when of a sudden Mister Lang and the boys in D3 let loose with a blast, the very one they been told to hold up on but never got the word, thanks to there bein' a jonah no doubt.

"Well, that blast was a good'un, boys, an' it threw all four of us arse over teakettle. Or leastways three of us, cuz when the dust settled, as they says, Murphy's there but Jones weren't nowhere ta be seen. And there, where he'd last been spied runnin' up the tunnel, was nothin' but a great heap a rock, filling up that tunnel like it was never dug out at all.

"Now as you might guess, me an' Murphy and the other man hightailed it right outta there, not waitin' around fer the rock ta bury us alongside John Jones, an' we figgered that was the end of it, and for once the jonah had got the bitter end. Only before much of an hour had gone, men was sent back down the D line to shore it up, since the Ds was still profitable in the eyes a the cap'n, and the men gone down there swears they hears noises over their radios. Cryin' and wailin' noises, sad 'n' terrible noises they were, or so they says. The rest of us thought they'd gone buggy, what with losin' a man so near ta hand an' all, even if he were a jonah. But then Perkins got to hearin' it when he come to inspect the shorin' up work, and right away he set the men ta dig out that cave-in, as he figgered Jones must still be alive, else who was doin' all that awful wailin'?

"So we digs out the spur—took most of another hour with four men at it, myself bein' one a them, an' we all figgered Jones fer dead in any case, for while we was about diggin', the wailin' had ceased. We dug and pitched over rocks an' when we'd cleared it all away, much to our surprise there weren't no body under there. I was right there, an' I c'n swear ta it if ya like. An' da ya know what was on t'other side a that rockfall, shipmates?" No one said a word. "Nothin', that's what. Not a single God fersaken thing, an' the spur a dead end." There was a respectful silence then, as the miners pondered Jones's fate. Chalk finished with the canonical conclusion for all ghost stories, be they terrestrial, maritime, or interplanetary in origin. "And ya know, shipmates, if'n ya goes down into ol'

D2 an' turns up the receiver on yer gear, I 'spect you'll hear the wailin' a John Jones even now."

This was an interesting tale, with a satisfactorily ambiguous termination, as well as an edifying message for the hearer. The moral, as I interpreted it, was to steer clear of a jonah, if you could, and if you couldn't, make certain at least that you were not him.

Chapter Four

Much of our time, when we were not busy lugging a hod through a succession of tunnels, was spent in the communal cavern known, thanks to the former whalers, as "belowdecks," or simply "below," despite the fact that it was actually above the rest of the mine. Only the depot where the ore carts were loaded was at a higher elevation. I called this homey space a cavern, but that word, humble as it is, still lends the belowdecks a grandeur it cannot live up to. It was a hole blasted out of the rock, like every other place men have contrived to live in the Moon, only smaller.

Nine men, including Bemis and myself, occupied this entrenchment, usually all nine of us at the same time. If occupancy had been organized as it was aboard a whaling ship or a man o' war, half the Deirdre's complement would have slept in the canopy of hammocks attached to the ceiling, while the other half worked, and then exchanged places—but there weren't enough experienced men to direct two shifts, let alone the three that were maintained by the Company in their strip mining operations, so the belowdecks seemed always to be either devoid of life, excepting the mine's cat and the occasional cockroach, or else full to bursting with humanity. Perhaps the cockroaches, those most tenacious of camp followers for the human race, swarmed over the belowdecks in our absence, but if so they were shy, and only a handful were generally available for our entertainment when we returned. And when we did return, we were a humanity fresh, if that is the word, from four hours of arduous toil, each man encased in his own canvas haggis and accumulating within it his own foul juices and noxious effluvia, and all of it was released into the same small space at more or less the same time. But since everyone but Mister Kent and Mister Lovelace, who ruled their own separate domains, had been out in the tunnels and sealed into their pressure suits, there was no one to complain of the sudden onslaught of stench and perspiration and too-long-sequestered human waste, because belowdecks was a paradise when compared to inhabiting your pressure suit.

This was due in no small part to the fact that the belowdecks was warm, when it wasn't stiflingly hot, and enjoyed a humidity that would make the jungles of Borneo green with envy. Mister Lovelace and his precious resonance engine, with all its accompanying devices that kept us alive, were located only a dozen yards beneath us, and the surplus steam from its boilers was enough to poach us like a school of catfish in a hot spring. It was glorious, and even cleansing after a fashion. The red Indian's sweat lodge had nothing on the belowdecks, except perhaps more elbow room.

It goes without saying perhaps, but I shall say it anyway, that a man's pressure suit, with its many parts—exterior skin, interior lining laced with heat producing wires, helmet, hoses, air cylinders, air regulator, batteries, water reservoir, gloves, boots, and various other parts either too gruesome or demoralizing to mention—was as important to a man's survival as his own skin, only more so. A lot of fuss was made in the Deirdre about maintaining one's pressure gear in prime, or at least adequate, working order, and much of the time spent belowdecks (after eating, sleeping, sweating, swearing, and the disposal of bodily wastes) was spent in the maintenance of it.

The attitude of the management with respect to suit maintenance was markedly different in the Deirdre than what we had known at Lunar Consolidated Mines. In the Deirdre, a man was expected to check each item of his gear, in a specific order and with well-delineated procedures, and effect any needed repairs himself, or if the job was beyond him, with the help of a mate. The Company had not been nearly so finicky. If a picker didn't maintain his gear, and the gear then went to its destruction, the picker got a new pressure suit for his trouble, at the full market price, assuming he was lucky enough to survive to pay for it. More often, a new picker was required along with the new set of gear. A while back I discussed how they disliked freelance terpsichore in the Company on account of the cost in pressure suits, and a taste for consistency might lead one to think that the maintenance of one's equipment would be encouraged for the same reason. And it was, but not if it cut into the time a man could spend working—which it would unless the niceties, such as eating and sleeping, were curtailed—and so, like temperance, Christian charity, and the brotherhood of man, proper suit maintenance was praised whenever it was mentioned, and otherwise ignored. But new, that is to say still living, men were harder to come by in the remote neighborhood of Farley's Crater, so all in the Deirdre were encouraged, not to say pressed, into performing regular maintenance on their gear.

The former whalers among us called the time set aside for this work "make 'n' mend," and it was as sacred, regular, and full of pomp and circumstance as high mass in the Vatican. For example, some things had to be done after every foray into the tunnels. Batteries must be reinvigorated, air cylinders and water reservoir refilled, liquid waste decanted, and dust removed from all of the more delicate, and vital, parts of one's suit, such as heat radiators, air valves, the helmet, glove, and boot seals, and the faceplate.

This pernicious dust was our constant companion in the Moon, a houseguest that, once allowed through the front door and installed in the spare bedroom, decides never to leave, and worse, never to leave you alone. He takes full possession of the sofa, gets familiar with every article of your food, backs up the plumbing, makes unreasonable demands on the servants, relentlessly monopolizes your leisure time, and works himself into the most recondite corners of your personal affairs. He never offers to take out the garbage, for he *is* the garbage, and never takes a day off to visit the circus or the undertaker to give you some relief from his constant presence. He is your faithful companion and, in his eyes at least, your dearest friend, and he would rather die the slow and painful death he deserves than leave you in peace. The only solution to a houseguest like this is to insist he seek a promotion and become a congressman, where he can stick his nose into everyone's business and eat them out of house and home wholesale, and for a living. The only solution for the dust is to root it out from wherever it is hiding and toss it into the street, with prejudice. Any luggage can be sent on later.

Along with everything else, the entire exterior skin of one's suit needed to be carefully inspected, as even the smallest tear, puncture, frayed seam, or deep abrasion could result in a loss of pressure. This was not a fatal calamity if the leak was a slow one and you were close to home, that is the belowdecks, but it could be a death sentence if you were, say, deep in the catacombs of D3 carrying out a hod full of ore. Unfortunately, I learned this lesson the hard way.

"Sam," said Bemis, "Don't look now, but I think you're pruning." We were heading up-tunnel, taking the last of the ore from a played-out spur. Bemis was at the aft end of the hod, as usual, and thus he had a fine view of the rear of my haggis over the top of the ore. This arrangement was not the result of bullying, trickery, or even heartfelt pleading on my part, although I was prepared to deploy all of these and more, had the need arisen. But as it happened Calvin actually preferred the aft position, or claimed he did, because he disliked maintaining the contortions necessary to grip the sticks low down behind him, as was often required on an up-tunnel run, quite as much as I disliked dodging whatever rocks might decide to abandon the hod. So, like Jack Sprat and his wife, we had discovered a comfortable division of labor that suited us both.

I began my response with an expletive, then said, "Are you sure?"

"Your, well, your arse is starting to pucker. It's hard to miss." The backside of one's pressure suit below the air cylinders was often the canary in the coal mine when it came to detecting a slow decompression. The area is broad regardless of one's physique, uncluttered, and unlike other more delicate parts of your haggis, has little to do except hold in air.

I said, "How bad is it, do you think?"

"If I can see it, I expect it's bad enough."

The stretch of tunnel we were in was, as usual, about as roomy as a corset on a sow. It would have been no trouble at all for an ambitious piece of rock to reach out and snag my suit. The only difficulty would be in deciding which of a thousand such rocks had got the contract for the work.

"Hell and damnation," I said. "So much for the slush." Some of the men smeared handfuls of fat, which they called "slush," provided by Mister Kent from the galley free of charge, onto the outsides of their pressure suits, in a fair imitation of a greased pig at a county fair. This would demonstrate an admirable level of ingenuity for a pig, in my opinion, but is less impressive in a miner, and I had only recently and reluctantly applied my first coat. The idea was to slip along through the tunnels like an oyster slides down one's gullet, but the practice stuck in my craw. Haggises are meant to be greasy, I suppose, but the effectiveness of the technique was questionable, as this incident proves, and once applied, the rancid fat became part of your suit for life.

"There's a junction up ahead, I think," said I, peering into the dark. This was indeed the case—it was the estimable D3-4, so at least we knew where we were—and we set the hod down in its mouth. Then we, and particularly Bemis, who had a better view of my more recondite parts than I, began to inspect the surface of my suit for signs of a leak. These deadly wellsprings of life-sustaining air were not easy to find in the dark, or under any conditions really, and none showed themselves in a cursory inspection. That was good news for me. The air inside of one's haggis was invariably thick with perspiration and other vapors that would spew out and crystalize in the vacuum, creating a small geyser. If such a geyser was easy to see, its owner was in serious peril—but to my great relief, Calvin reported no geysers.

Still, the leak must be found. The accepted technique for this added insult to injury, but was otherwise reasonably effective. It consisted in throwing handfuls of our friend the dust at each portion of one's suit in turn, and watching, in the criss-crossed beams of your partner's and your helmet lamps, for the dust to jump away from the surface of the suit as it was disturbed by the air escaping from a (hopefully minuscule) hole in the fabric. The technique still worked even if you had been foolish enough to slather your haggis with slush, but if you had, then the majority of the dust stuck to the fat, and this was yet another strike against its application. The combination of dust and animal fat was a union made in Hades, and putting the two together was like having a lifelong houseguest who brings with him a large, hungry, and bumptious goat. While dust by itself can, with much effort and tenacity, be removed from the cracks, crevices, and cul de sacs of one's suit, any grease in the vicinity will come to its aid and seal it in place. The viscidity of the villainous compound thus created is remarkable. Only precious soap and water freely and wantonly applied will touch it, and even with that formidable posse on its trail it is nearly impossible to dislodge.

So by the time the leak was discovered, I was thoroughly tarred and feathered, and by my own hand. Given my keen ability to find, if not court, trouble wherever it sought to roam, I had expected to be the guest of honor at a good tar-and-feathering, even one with torches and a rail, before I'd got too old and set in my ways to enjoy it, but I had never expected to have to perform the necessary ablutions for myself. It would take ages to scrape the muck from the skin of my suit, but as it turned out I would have ample time for the job.

At last, a plume of dust rose from my right knee joint. "Got it!" I said, then sprinkled more dust over the accordion folds to refine the search.

Calvin stopped throwing dust at me then and crouched over the knee. "Seam's torn on the third fold," he said. This was a popular spot at which to damage one's suit, as hod carrying often found one on gloves and knees in those narrow, sloping tunnels. Bemis paused for a distressing few moments, then said, "We can't patch that out here, Sam. It'll have to be sewn up and tarred."

"Ah, there ya be," came a voice, torn apart with static but still recognizable.

"Who's that?" Bemis said. "Is that Chalk?"

"Aye, 'tis Chalk, shipmates." A wandering beam of light flashed from somewhere down the throat of

D3-4. "I was comin' up the D3 when I hear the two a ya talking 'bout a hole in yer suit. When I hears that sorta talk, boys, I come a runnin'. Where's she spoutin'?"

"The right knee," Bemis said. "Top of the fold."

Chalk bent to peer at the tiny gash, then clucked his tongue. "Bad place fer a tear, that is. No way to close that short a the belowdecks. An' walkin' on it 'll jus' tear it worse." Gottschalk was a font of good news, I thought, like the obituary page.

"So what can I do?" I croaked.

"Nothin'" he said.

"Nothing?" I repeated. I could hear the fear in my voice.

"Jus' you set still, now. Calvin an' me 'll bring ya in." He drew a short length of rope from somewhere. "I seen men with worse that lived ta tell the tale." He wrapped the rope around the top fold of the knee joint, then pulled it tight, painfully tight, and secured it with a mysterious seaman's knot.

"Uh," I said through a growing pain in my knee, "are you sure that's a good idea, Chalk?"

"Only thing for it, mate. Ya gotta stop the air from gettin' out, now don'cha?"

"But it didn't hurt 'til you tied it off," I insisted.

"Hurtin's a good sign, way I sees it. Means yer gam there is still alive. When ya cain't feel 'er no more, that's when there's cause ta worry, ya see." He flicked a gloved finger against my thigh. A hollow thud echoed up from within my suit. "Fine. That's holdin', ain't it."

"What about my leg?" I said.

"Ah, don't you worry, Samuel. Like I said, I seen worse. Had a deuce of a time with Peterson at first, as I recall, but he come out well enough." I wondered how well was well enough, but said nothing. "That were most of a year ago now, I reckon. He was fine, by an' large. Leastways he were after the surgery."

"Surgery?" I squeaked.

"Now, Calvin, you help him ta stand up, and mind the leg. I'll not be responsible for what happens if that line was to come loose." He pointed at the rope. Then he addressed me. "I tol' ya, Samuel, you rest easy." Apparently I was supposed to rest easy while I got to my feet and, presumably, climbed the tunnel. "There ain't a thing ta worry about. Mister Kent, he's a wizard with the saw."

"Saw?" I whimpered.

"Sure's yer born, ol' son. As I recollects, Peterson was his old self again inside a month." Chalk chuckled as he led the way up-tunnel. "Not quite all his old self, a course," he added ominously. "He weren't up ta totin' hod no more, it's true, but—"

"My leg is getting cold," I said. "Very cold." It also hurt like the devil, but I figured that was old news.

"Course it is. That's the next thing happens, ya see. But don'cha worry now, Samuel. Peterson got along jus' fine, he did, though it's true a peg's something of a nuisance in a pressure suit."

"Peg?" I sobbed.

"Yup, 'twere a fine one, too. Mister Lovelace he made it from a length a pipe. Were right proud of it, he was. Now, Calvin, you lifts Samuel's leg over whilst I pulls him up." I was being hoisted over one of the steeper points of D3. When the tunnel was more navigable again, Chalk asked casually, "And how's the gam then?" The pain had vacated my leg below the knee and had lodged in my thigh. It was excruciating even at that remove. I now felt nothing below the tourniquet.

"It's fine," I said, whistling a chorus of Yankee Doodle as I passed the graveyard. "The thigh hurts, but I don't feel a thing below the knee."

Chalk said nothing for a long moment, but he clucked several times, which was worse. Then he said, "Yer vacuum 'll do that, it will. Nothin' for it. But don't ya worry none. Men rarely dies from such a thing. Leastways most of 'em." I was spared the remainder of Chalk's opinions, because when he bent to tighten the rope around my leg, I passed out.

I awoke in the airlock when Calvin took my helmet off, but I said nothing and kept my eyes closed, and continued to do so for the remainder of the trip to Mister Kent's lair. I decided to play possum for two reasons: to take advantage of what I considered a well deserved opportunity for sloth—

being carried through a tunnel like a hodful of ore made for a strangely pleasant, if bumpy, ride—and to gather information. In my experience, people are reluctant to tell you to your face that you are going to die, at least if you're scheduled to do it any time soon, and if I was slated to expire, say, before supper, I wanted to know it. I reckoned I might have a good deal of explaining to do to get inside the Pearly Gates, and I needed some time to polish up my material.

This worked about as well as could be expected. No one said I was about to die, but then no one said I wasn't either. No one said anything of significance during the whole trip. That is, no one said anything about me.

I kept my eyes shut even when we reached the sickbay. It smelled like mutton stew that day, although I couldn't imagine where they'd find any mutton, except perhaps salted away in a hogshead. I was placed on a bed hastily assembled from foodstuffs, and almost immediately heard Mister Kent invoke the Deity, and not in a kindly way. I thought, perhaps they will let me have a plate of that mutton stew before I die.

Then he said, "Damn you, Chalk. This is some of your work, i'n't it?"

"Aye, Mister Kent."

"Well, he'll be lucky if he doesn't lose the leg, thanks to you."

Chalk said, "It's the only way I know's ta —"

Kent cut him off. "It i'n't a shark bite, you fool." He sighed. "There's likely to be significant vacuum trauma."

"Twas only tryin' ta help, Mister Kent."

"Yes, yes, I know. Now run along. And you too, Bemis. You're no use here." Then Kent said, "And you, Clemens. Quit pretending you're unconscious." I opened my eyes. "That's better. Now hold still while I untie this line." I looked down the length of my haggis to assay the extent of the damage and saw his scarred hands reaching for the knot. "This is likely to hurt a bit, but it'll pass soon enough."

The rope line came loose from the suit's knee joint and soon I felt a tingling sensation in the lower part of my leg. "It's fine," I said. "Not so bad, just a sort of— yaaaw!" I cried out as a sudden horrible aching pain engulfed my leg below the knee.

"Rest easy, son. It'll pass," Kent said again.

"When?" I said through gritted teeth.

"Hard to say."

Kent slowly removed the lower portion of my pressure suit. He *tsk*ed and shook his head, his great red beard waggling, as he inspected my leg, which was now turned a dreadful purplish blue, like a carcass of meat left in the snow. "In a few hours, I expect."

"A few *hours*?" Apparently I wasn't going to die after all, but now I regretted the fact. "Are you going to saw off my leg?" The pain being what it was, I decided I was in favor of the procedure, but only if death was no longer an option.

The beard waggled again. "D'rather not. It's a messy business, and some say it can hurt a bit." He inspected my foot then. "This toe is going to have to come off, however." Then a moment later, "No. It's done the work for us and come off by itself." I felt a lightning bolt of pain, sauce for the main course the rest of the leg was serving, and then Kent held up an inch-long gobbet of my very own flesh, now lost to me forever under my very eyes. There was no fakery this time, and I fainted, again.

Chapter Five

Mister Kent was kind enough to offer me the vacuum-frozen toe for a souvenir, but I declined the gift, mostly because I had no place to keep it, except attached to my foot. Failing that, I was indifferent to the disposition of the remains, asking only that it not be fed to the Deirdre's cat, or anyone else, for a snack. I expect that to this day it resides in a jar of mineral spirits somewhere inside the Moon.

The pain in my leg was fairly horrible for most of a week. There was no cure for this, apparently, though whiskey, then going for three dollars and twenty-five cents an ounce in Captain Merriwether's ledger, offered it some competition, and I ran up my bill, and the length of my term of servitude, accordingly. I bet on the whiskey, repeatedly, with the dogged, forlorn desperation of a racetrack punter already deep in the hole, but the pain was too much for it and took home the purse every time. Only sleep, in whose depths all sensation vanishes, provided genuine relief. Still, the whiskey hangovers I awoke with were useful; they stood in and provided some misery while the real pain woke up and got its britches on.

The first few days of my convalescence, I was confined to the sickbay, and whenever I was not sprawled in a hammock luxuriating in my agony, I spent the time repairing my pressure suit. Fixing the hole in the knee joint, although exacting, was far easier than removing the concoction of grease and dust from the suit's exterior, which was nearly impossible. But as it happened, like any number of things, whiskey was the cure for it. I suppose you think I mean the drinking of it, and it's true that this was a slight help in combating the tedium that came with the project, but it also had a most salubrious effect upon the stubborn muck itself. It seemed that the slush did not appreciate its society, and fled from it like the whiskey was carrying a warrant for its arrest, and the dust came along as an accomplice. Once I discovered this miracle, my term of servitude increased again.

It took two full days, minus the time spent sleeping, suffering, imbibing whiskey, and sleeping again, before the cleaning and repairing was complete. (I knew how much time was passing thanks to Mister Lovelace's clock with the truncated pendulum, whose electrically relayed chimes, sounding in imitation of a ship's bells, echoed through the parts of the Deirdre that possessed air. This was Earthbound time of course, and bore as much resemblance to the actual passage of days and nights on the Moon as a Fiji witch-doctor does to Queen Victoria, but it told me when supper was due and that was enough.) Once my gear was back in shape, there was very little for me to do, and in spite of my lifelong dedication to the vice of sloth, I grew bored.

To ameliorate this, I offered to help Mister Kent with the cooking, once he had agreed to let me stand upright for brief spells. This was a more than serviceable diversion, and I enjoyed it while it lasted. But it was too choice a berth to hold for long, I suppose. On only the third day of my apprenticeship, while rummaging about the galley in Mister Kent's absence, I came across a trunk full of wonderful condiments and exotic spices. These marvelous additives proved irresistible, and before I knew it, improvisation had got the better of me and I produced a stew that even Puss, the mine's cat, who was widely known and admired for her catholic tastes, would not touch. I was proud of my work in this new vocation, and thought less of Puss for her opinion. For my part, I thought it fine, though admittedly pungent. It went down largely without incident if you didn't slow it down by trying to chew it, and tasted almost like proper stew if you thought to hold your nose. I was shocked, and disappointed of its further use, when Mister Kent informed me, rather hotly as I remember, that the trunk contained as many articles of physic, such as skin liniment, poultices, and draughts for the relief of constipation as it did condiments, and in his opinion I had employed more than the necessary amount of each in seasoning my concoction.

Bemis came to visit me fairly often, which helped with the boredom. Since I was laid up with an injured limb, it appeared that my partner in hod toting was at loose ends. This seemed a strange lacuna in an enterprise that wanted men, any men, badly enough to lurk in the rim of Farley's Crater, like a spider in her web, ready to rouse them out of the dust. But according to Calvin, all of the ore, and even the lion's share of the tailings, had been removed from the Deirdre for the moment, and thus the hods stood idle. He said word around the belowdecks was that a major new shaft was to be sunk, or blasted out with explosives rather, in an attempt to reveal a new, voluminous, and superior cache of ice. So Bemis, at leisure for pretty much the first time since I'd known him, had taken up with Mister Lovelace, and spent hours in his chambers beneath the belowdecks, where the heat and humidity were truly astonishing, communing with the resonance engine and the other wondrous devices it supported. Not long after the incident with the stew, I was encouraged to visit him there, the only proviso being that I should keep off the injured leg as much as possible.

The pain in the limb gradually subsided, more or less in concert with the consumption of whiskey, I'll confess. However, no sooner had it become bearable than a new phenomenon came calling, one which I thought an unnecessary extravagance. The toe, or at least the sensations available through it, which I had thought lost to oblivion with the departure of the organ itself, was suddenly returned to me, with a vengeance. I could see the sorry appendage floating disconsolately, if not insolently, in a jar in Mister Kent's sickbay, yet it nevertheless insisted on itching, burning, tingling, and aching as if it were still attached to my foot, and not living there in contentment either. It behaved as if it resented the vacuum freezing and wanted revenge, and it got it too. I'd heard of this phenomenon, sometimes called the phantom limb, from men who had lost an arm or a leg in battle, but I had always taken their descriptions of these ghostly, inexplicable sensations to be instances of poetic license. That is, I thought they were lying. I know now that they were not, and if anything were understating the case. As it is, I can only hope I don't misplace any more body parts, especially major ones, for if I did, I think their constant complaining would drive me to distraction.

I had not visited Mister Lovelace's domain prior to my convalescence, and at first did not know how even to get there until I hobbled over to the belowdecks and asked around. Most of the men, including Perkins, Chalk, Winters, Garrett, and Watkins were there, lounging in their hammocks in the steamy gloom, playing poker, or tending to the insatiable needs of their pressure suits. I had not been back into the belowdecks since my haggis had sprung a leak, and the men would not hear a word from me until I had rolled up my overalls and presented the injured limb for inspection. And they were right to do so, for, although according to Mister Kent the limb was sound, it, or what was left of it, made for a spectacular show, and if I had been prescient enough to charge admission to see it, I expect I could have paid for my extra whiskey outright. Thanks to the vacuum, the limb was decorated from the knee to the four remaining toes in a gaudy, livid, multihued bruise that would have put a week-old cadaver to shame. I turned this marvel to and fro, displaying every patch of purple, green, yellow, blue, and black to its full effect, and all but the severest of the former whalers lavished the most satisfying compliments upon it.

To my dismay, Chalk was niggardly in his praise for the limb, saying merely, "I seen worse," by which he meant more spectacularly horrific, I suppose.

"Not on a man that kept the leg, I'll wager," countered Watkins. I thanked him, in my thoughts anyway, for his support of the abused limb.

Such a concise evaluation, of anything, was not in Chalk's nature as I had observed it, and it occurred to me that his reluctance to lavish the gam with the praise it deserved might stem from some lingering sense of responsibility for its present condition, but in the end I believe he was simply envious of its undeniable splendor. Alas, even the best of us may fall silent when placed nose-to-nose with the sublime.

Eventually, once the show had let out and my pants leg was restored, I mentioned that I was looking for Bemis and expected to find him with Mister Lovelace in his lair. Then I asked Perkins, who was beside me, how I might get there.

"Go on down the rabbit hole," he said with a grin. "Just follow the steam and you can't miss it." And he pointed to a short passage that was dripping with condensation.

"Down the rabbit hole?" I scoffed, looking around the belowdecks. "I could have sworn I was there already."

Nevertheless, I went into the opening indicated, and it was a good thing I was hobbling along like a lamed mule or I would have arrived in Mister Lovelace's realm with a broken neck, because the way through to the place was nothing but a yawning shaft sunk straight down into the rock. There was no ladder of any description leading into it, only a cluster of pipes coming up out of the hole, along with several fat bundles of insulated wires, which presumably took electrical energy to the various parts of the Deirdre to feed the electric lights and the battery charging devices in the belowdecks.

I leant forward, bracing myself on my whole left leg, and peered into the shaft. It was a modest four feet or so in diameter, but could have been a thousand feet deep for all I could see of the bottom of it. The only signs that it had an end anywhere this side of eternity were the cloud of steam rising from it, and a dense, rumbling cacophony of mechanical sounds.

Still leaning forward, I called down into the hole over the distant racket, shouting, "Calvin? Calvin Bemis, are you in there?"

There was no reply, so I repeated the call. I waited a moment longer, then at last a voice rose out of the depths, saying something that was largely unintelligible. Whether it was the voice of Bemis or Lovelace I could not tell, but somewhere in the jumble of words penetrating the general din I heard the command to "come ahead," or anyway I fancied I did. I stared down into that abyss and pondered how I was to go about that, when the voice returned with the mysterious injunction to "use the pole." It was then that I noticed that there was indeed a thick aluminum pole starting in the roof and disappearing down into the blackness. I had thought this merely another pipe sending air to some distant cavern, such as Captain Merriwether's cabin, and, although wrong, this was a worthy assumption, because of course it was a pipe, only one set to a different purpose. It crossed my mind that, had I been a bit more thorough in arranging my recent calamity, I would have found a section of just such a pipe strapped to the stump of my leg.

I considered protesting this overly precipitous mode of transportation, but knew from the nature of the conversation so far that no one below would be likely to understand me if I did, so I drew in a deep breath, grabbed the pole with both hands, stepped into the void, and slid down into the hole. The trip did not last long, fortunately, as the shaft was only about thirty feet deep. That would have been plenty long enough to break a man's leg on Earth, even with the pole for assistance, but it was only a modest plunge as such things are reckoned on the Moon. Still, I had the presence of mind to take the landing on my good leg alone, otherwise I expect I would be howling in pain to this day.

Once I was again on solid ground, I began to look around, and saw all about me a bewildering collection of machinery, seemingly all of it in fervent, not to say frenetic, motion. Gleaming rods thrust pistons in and out of their cylinders, gears racketed around their shafts, pulleys pulled, fly wheels flew, and gouts of steam belched from more orifices than I cared to count. A low, steady rumbling filled the cavern, accompanied by a clattering and banging like a whole kitchen-full of pots and pans being thrown repeatedly down the basement stairs. All around me, and even above me, the machinery sat—the parts that weren't in wild motion anyway—looming like great prehistoric beasts wreathed in clouds of steam. This steam was penetrated in ghostly fashion by no less than three electric bulbs hanging on wires above the machines. Three electric lights in a single space set a new record, and Mister Kent with his brace of two was suddenly knocked down a step in my pantheon.

"Sam!" called Bemis from somewhere in the chaos of flailing pistons and whirring gears, "I'm so glad you're here." He poked his grease and sweat-smeared face out from behind a clutch of cogs (or perhaps sprockets, assuming there's a difference), and I waved and smiled my respects. "How's the leg today?" he added.

"Fair to middling," I said with a shrug.

"How's that?" he hollered over the noise.

"Splendid," I tried. In fact, the absent toe was itching like the devil, but that was far too much information for this sort of conversation.

"Good," Bemis said, then, "Say, could you hand me up a spanner?"

I glanced about me in an effort to locate the article, but could see nothing that fit my idea of such a device. Before I could admit defeat, Mister Lovelace appeared beside me with the requested tool. I took it from him as if I'd been waiting on it all afternoon, then reached up and shoved it into Calvin's outstretched hand. He thanked me, then was gone again behind the housing of a collection of gears.

"Your friend Bemis is a good mechanic," said Lovelace over the pounding of the machines. "He's still rather light on theory and wants a good deal of experience yet, but I expect that in time he'll make a first-rate resonance engineer."

This was news to me, and not exactly welcome news either. "That may be, sir," I said, "I am certainly no judge of ability when it comes to engineers, but he and I are out here for the prospecting. The Deirdre is merely a way station to that end."

Somewhat to my relief he did not laugh, but only smiled. "And that may be as well, Clemens, but surely it is evident—" he spared me the 'even to you' that the remark craved "—that the ability to operate a resonance engine and its peripheral machinery is essential to any serious mining endeavor in the Moon." He swept his arm through the air, encompassing all the mechanisms surrounding us. "Indeed, the digging leviathan you arrived in is nothing but the scaled down equivalent of what you see before you." I wanted to speak up for the Beast and point out that there was also its great digging claw to consider, and I saw no such apparatus among the boilers and pistons in there, but Bemis took that moment to reappear, then hop down to the floor of the cavern in front of us.

He turned to me and crowed, "Ain't it a beauty, Sam? She has ten times the capacity of the Beast's engine, and—"

"Oh, considerably more than that, I should think," Lovelace said.

"Certainly," I said. "I'll not deny it's an estimable pile, and no doubt insatiable as well, but then there's no digging claw, is there? That does the business I came for."

Bemis and Lovelace both laughed, apparently considering this an attempt at humor on my part, instead of God's honest truth.

Bemis glanced at Lovelace then, and Lovelace nodded in response. Then Bemis took two strides to a big panel and threw open several pairs of large knife blade switches. Miniature bolts of lightning jumped across the gaps as he did so, and Calvin quickly drew his hands away. Immediately the great machines around me began to slow their hectic motion, and after about a minute they had stopped completely. The ensuing silence was, as they say, deafening. Then Calvin turned to his mentor and asked, with all the solemnity and barely suppressed excitement proper to a ten-year-old boy asking permission to take his little sister to see the dog-faced boy, if he might show me the sacred interior of the resonance engine itself.

Permission was granted, and he led me over to a vessel the size of a large boiler, but substantially more convoluted, with several access hatches, one of which he un-dogged and threw open with a flourish. He took a headlamp of the kind we used on our pressure helmets, with its battery strapped to its side with a length of cable, and shone it into the hatch.

Peering inside the vessel I saw, amidst a latticework of supports, three life preserver rings of three different diameters nested one inside the other and canted at odd angles to one another.

"Those are the very electromagnetic coils themselves," he said. "If the engine was operating, they would be spinning of course, at various rates and at different angles depending on which sorts of molecules we were trying to dissociate."

I knew that dissociating molecules, by which the savants meant separating them into their component atoms, was the primary business of a resonance engine. "Certainly it is—they do," I said. "You mean those life preservers, I suppose."

He laughed. "I guess they do look like life preservers, but I wouldn't want to throw one at a drowning man. They're almost solid copper, and if it were not for the Faraday shielding they'd flood the aether with very hazardous vibrational energies as they spin." I peered in at the copper coil life preservers with reinvigorated interest, as any emergency flotation device that also emits hazardous vibrational energies surely deserves respect. "Fortunately, you came at the perfect time to see them. The engine is only idle because we are—" he looked deferentially at Mister Lovelace, who was standing with arms folded across his overalls listening to Calvin recite "—because Mister Lovelace is about to switch her over to dissociating cee-oh-two." I feared that he was about to tell me that CO_2

stood for carbon dioxide, and brand me an imbecile in the process, but he didn't.

Next to the vacuum itself, which is actually nothing at all and thus exceedingly hard to reason with, carbon dioxide is the vilest enemy of the men in the Moon. It is, if you did not know it, an invisible gas deadly to human and animal life when breathed exclusively, as you will do inside your pressure suit once your air is exhausted. Men claim that dying in this way is not unpleasant, that it is in fact quite pleasurable, but despite these reviews I am reluctant to try it. This behavior is sufficiently evil all by itself to earn the molecule the Moon dweller's respect, and enthusiastic condemnation, but its ignominy is increased still further when you consider its origin. For of course its source is none other than ourselves. Along with the usual dunnage of nitrogen, it is carbon dioxide that we expel from our lungs once the air we breathe is relieved of its oxygen. It is one thing to be slowly poisoned by an invisible gas, and another to know that you have produced that poison yourself.

"May I set the angles of inclination, Mister Lovelace?" Bemis asked.

"Certainly. Do you remember the proper order?"

"Inner to outer," he said with confidence.

"Quite so," Lovelace agreed.

I watched as Calvin turned a succession of small wheels mounted on the exterior of the chamber, which in turn caused the shining life preservers to change their orientation with respect to each other. The positions were then adjusted to a great precision with the aid of verniers mounted at the bottom of each wheeled dial. I would attempt to explain to you how a vernier does its work, but as I suspect it is a form of black magic, I have stayed ignorant of the details in order to keep my accounts book clean with the Almighty. Nevertheless, the vernier provides an accuracy of measurement beyond human ken, and engineers and other practitioners of the black arts find them indispensable to their work.

So Calvin adjusted the dials using the little wheels, then had a bout with each of the three verniers, squinting at them suspiciously and counting quietly to himself. Finally, he stepped back and allowed Mister Lovelace to inspect his work. No correction was required, and Bemis, renewed in his enthusiasm, went on to worry more dials and invoke more verniers as he set the rate of rotation for each of the copper life preservers within, saying, "If you do it right, the carbon atoms will dissociate from the oxygen and you have the makings of fresh air again."

"Marvelous," I intoned. "I'm four square in favor of fresh air. But where is the resonance? Will I get a peek at that? They talk it up like a dime stock going on sale for a penny, but I'd like to see a slice of it, or at least get taken to see where it lives."

Calvin laughed and Lovelace smiled his inscrutable smile.

"Why, resonance isn't a thing, Sam, it's a, well—" He glanced once again at Lovelace, but his sage left him to dig out by himself. "—it's a process," he decided. "It's why a bridge will shake apart if the men going across it march in step." I looked at him with incredulity, but said nothing, as the statement, as well as its possible relevance, was incomprehensible to me. But he plunged ahead anyway, saying, "In any case, the rotating electromagnetic coils create a succession of electromagnetic waves that interfere with each other in such a way as to—" Again he looked to Lovelace for help but was stoically denied. "—to create waves of a specific energy, which when inflicted on the molecules of CO_2, causes them to, well, to vibrate so violently that they come apart into their constituent atoms. And with only a tiny amount of electrical energy expended to do it. That's what makes it such a boon to mankind," he concluded. There is theory enough beneath this claim to float a university in, and none of it comprehensible to a soul except the great Tesla, and perhaps his partner Faraday, so I shan't trouble you with it here.

"But where is the resonance?" I insisted. "What happened to that?"

Calvin tried not to look disappointed, and failed. "That is the resonance," he insisted right back.

I shook my head to clear away some of the science and leave room for honest thought. "Never mind,

Calvin. But you said 'if you do it right' before. What if you do it wrong?"

"Then it doesn't work," he said matter-of-factly.

Mister Lovelace released a snort.

"Unless of course you do it very wrong," he amended. I said nothing, waiting for the punchline. "Then it's liable to, well, explode."

"I see," I said, and I did. "That's why this monstrosity is far removed from the belowdecks then. With only a mouse hole to get in by."

Calvin shrugged. "Well, that's more in case of the boilers going up, which is far more likely."

"I see," I said again, and looked for something, anything, resembling an exit. "And I suppose the only way out is to climb that pole."

"Don't fret, Sam," he said. "It's perfectly safe." And he was right. It was no doubt perfectly safe, if you were somewhere else, preferably somewhere far away, like Philadelphia.

"And what happens to the carbon?" said I, wishing to be thorough in my confusion.

He grinned. "That's an excellent question, Sam. At present, nothing, which is a shame. It's the purest form of soot, you see, and it needs to be swept out regularly, like a chimney in the spring. But Mister Lovelace has been working on a method of capturing the carbon and forcing it to bond with itself in a, um —" He glanced at Lovelace yet again, but to no avail.

"—into a stable matrix. Do you know what that would yield, Sam?"

"Um, chocolate fudge?" I said, although I knew it was too good to be true.

He laughed and said, "Better than that." Once again I waited for the punchline. His grin stood out starkly against his dark face, and his eyes went wide. He obviously was convinced he had hold of a whopper, and was eager to land it in my boat. "Diamonds," he said at last, as if he'd spoken a holy thing.

"I see," I said, and once again I did. Clearly this was no place in which to find sober men. The resonance was loose, and hazardous vibrational energies filled more than just the aether, they had filled these men's heads with fantasies as well.

"It's only a theory and might not work at all," said Lovelace. He shooed the theory away with a wave of his hand, then addressed Bemis. "Close it up, son, and we'll show Clemens how we separate out the nitrogen and such. Would you like to see that, Mister Clemens?"

"I'm pleased to see anything," I said, "just as long as it's not about to explode." I thought this was innocent enough, and fairly clever too, but it was in fact an ill-timed and ill-considered remark, given what transpired in the ensuing days.

Chapter Six

There came a day, not long after my first visit to the den of the resonance engine, when Mister Kent declared me, or my leg at any rate, fit for duty, and I was permitted to shift my kit, mostly consisting of my dear haggis, back to the belowdecks, and resume my place in polite society. Calvin happened to be visiting the sickbay on that day and he congratulated me on a complete recovery, if returning one toe lighter can be considered a complete recovery. I was even allowed to don a full pair of boots for the occasion. I had been hobbling around lopsided for more than a week and was pleased to right the ship and walk like a Christian again.

I was just trying on the right boot, easing it on slowly lest it ignite the ire of the phantom toe, when Perkins and Captain Merriwether himself came through the aft tunnel.

"Well, Captain Merriwether and Mister Perkins," I said, "how good of you to visit me in my home away from home, far away from home." The two men only smiled, or Perkins did, but I steamed ahead anyway, adding, "This is taking on the look of a celebration. Shall we break out the whiskey and drink to my liberation from the sickbay by adding a week to my sentence?" The captain and Perkins demurred, so my term of servitude was not increased that day. It seemed that they were there on business, and not to toast to the health of my leg.

"I expect you've heard rumors," began Captain Merriwether, "that we intend to sink a new shaft."

"Splendid," I said. "That gets us all the way up to E in the alphabet."

"Don't interrupt, please, Clemens," said Perkins.

I resolved to obey this injunction, but somehow knew it wouldn't be easy.

The captain continued, "There is always the risk that it will not pan out, as the gold miners back on Earth like to say, but if it does then there should be a great deal of profit in it." I kept my mouth closed, but couldn't help wondering why a personage as august, and generally aloof, as Captain Merriwether would take the time to explain his plans to the likes of us, two mere hod carriers, and the two greenest men in the Deirdre, if not in all of the Moon. "If we make a sizable find, you men should be able to pay off your debt and start making a living for yourselves." I wondered why he was trying to sell us on a course of action he had clearly already decided upon.

Bemis, who had not technically been consigned to silence, was obviously thinking along the same lines, and he went directly to the heart of the matter. "And you would like us to participate," he said matter-of-factly.

Perkins, who looked unaccountably nervous, nodded in affirmation.

The captain, however, sailed on without any acknowledgement, saying, "There will be a good deal of work with explosives, including the sticks you fellows brought along, and thank you for that."

Now I was convinced. He wanted something from Calvin and me, but he already had us in his service, and willingly for the most part—so what more did he require?

"We don't have much experience with explosives," Calvin said, by which he meant none at all.

"Mister Lang and Perkins here will be handling the explosives," the captain said.

And Perkins, who was clearly in on this conspiracy, added, "You two can finally learn something about mining, if you pay attention." We couldn't help but learn something, I thought, since that hod sat all but empty as it was.

Although I had been told to keep my opinions to myself, I could stand it no longer, and I said, "I have no doubt you're right, Mister Perkins, but—" I turned to look at Merriwether "—Captain, the last time I checked, we were still at your service. Is there something particularly hazardous in this duty that you are not saying, besides the explosives, which requires that we volunteer?"

Perkins gave the captain a glance that told me I had struck ice. But, although my inquiry caused the captain to tack, it was not sufficient to cause him to heave to and let the cat out of its sack.

"Three of the men finished paying off their rescue some time ago, and they have taken this opportunity to return to Earth with what they have earned."

"Or to Lucky Strike anyway, where they can use a portion of it to buy a hot bath," Perkins added. That still left a handful of men more experienced at, well, at everything, than Calvin and myself. There was still a cat in the sack somewhere, or a boot still poised to drop, depending on your choice of metaphor, but I couldn't guess what it was.

Bemis, who despite all appearances, is smarter than I am, asked, "Where is the new shaft to be sunk?" And I could see immediately that it was Calvin who had truly struck ice, because both the captain and Perkins were visibly taken aback by his innocent-sounding question.

Captain Merriwether tried to skim over the shoal with, "Like Clemens says, it'll likely be designated as E."

Perkins, who saw the shoal more clearly, gave in and wore ship, saying, "There's no use trying to hide it, Captain. Boogerin' Chalk'll spill it to 'em anyhow, likely before they get their air cylinders out of the rack."

Merriwether sighed and turned into the wind. "We intend to blast further into D2. We want to explore down a spur that we think was abandoned too hastily before."

This meant nothing to me, although I suppose I'd been there once or twice toting hod, but before I could confess my ignorance, Perkins finally heaved around to the point.

"It's the spur where—where Jones was lost," he said at last, as if the admission explained everything, maybe even the Resurrection. "I'm sure Chalk, or someone, has told you about what happened to Jones."

"Oh yes," Bemis said, "the fellow who died mysteriously. The man who was considered—what do the sailors call it—a joshua?" Joshua? Oh, for Heaven's sake. And to think I had taken Calvin for a Baptist.

"Jonah," I corrected. "Yes. Chalk told us all about it, the poor fellow. But, honestly, it's the best ghost story I've heard since I left New Orleans." Although the fog was beginning to lift, I found that I still could not make out the point.

"Well," said the captain, "except for Garrett and Watkins, who we came by in a manner very similar to yourselves, the remaining men all came with us from the Deirdre—the original Deirdre, that is, which was a whaling vessel."

"I had wondered where the name came from," I confessed.

"Sailors, especially whaling men, are a superstitious lot," said Perkins. "And as ridiculous as it may sound, they'll have no part of that spur. Won't go near it for love or money. And said as much to the captain's face."

"Because a man died?" said Bemis. "A lot of men die in the Moon."

"No," said Perkins. "Not because he died. As you say, that's common enough out here. No, best I can figure it's because he is, was, a jonah. And because he didn't die clean. If he had, that would probably, almost certainly, have put an end to it, but the man just disappeared, or his corpse did in any case. It seems that the ghost of a jonah—" He gave up and shook his head. "Honestly, I'm not sure what the booger they believe, only they will have nothing to do with that section of D2, not even to tote hod."

"What about Watkins and Garrett?" I said.

Captain Merriwether sighed. "They've been infected by the others, I'm afraid. In their defense, they were here when Jones, um, met his fate. They didn't like it then and they don't like it now."

"Sounds like a mutiny," I said.

"Stow that, Clemens," Perkins said sharply.

I said, "My apologies, Captain." It occurred to me then that I had made a poor job of keeping my mouth closed.

Merriwether ignored my outburst, and my apology, saying instead, "So how about it, boys, will you help us dig out the new shaft, or are you afraid of ghosts like the other men?"

"I have no problem with it," Calvin said, "as I for one do not believe in ghosts. Except for the Holy Ghost, I suppose, but that's a different matter." I vowed to myself that one day I would get to the bottom of Calvin's religion, but not that day.

"And how about you, Clemens?" said Merriwether. "Are you willing?"

"Honestly, sir, I'm more afraid of the explosives going off half-cocked than I am of meeting a ghost. Being exploded seems a much more likely calamity to me."

"Does that mean you will do it then?"

"I suppose so. What will you be expecting us to do?"

"Tote your hod, mostly," Perkins said.

"Well, I'm up to that. Mostly," I said, waggling my celebrated limb.

"And help with the explosives some, if you're game," he added, daring me to stand my ground. "You'll never make a prospector if you can't handle explosives."

"And that's the truth," said Merriwether.

Perkins's harpoon had been well aimed, and it sunk into me tolerably deep. I either wanted to be a prospector and become rich on a diet of precious minerals and ice, or else I wanted to talk it to death and return home empty-handed, and one digit shy of a complete set.

I said, "Point made. Very well then. I am your huckleberry."

"I will take that for a yes," said the captain. "Be suited up and ready for vacuum at three bells. And don't let Chalk pour a load of bilge into your ears in the meantime."

We did as we were instructed, and I soon returned to the belowdecks with my pressure suit in tow. Since they had refused to work, all the former whalers were there, lounging in their hammocks, or else practicing the fantastic, heretical form of poker revealed to them through the necessity of playing with the Deirdre's sole, venerable, and deeply perverted pack of cards. I would like to say that those men were not playing with a full deck, but as satisfying as it would be to say it, it would not be the truth, for, if anything, the pack in question was overcrowded, like a barroom on election day. True, its roster was missing a number of prominent personages, including, as I recall, both the king and queen of diamonds and the jack of spades, but it made up for its low stock in royals by carrying three jokers, a spare trey, half a dozen nines, and a truly astonishing number of aces, most of which had been dogeared for easy identification. There were so many of these in fact that the "baby ticket," as the gamblers on the river sometimes called it, had to be played at a steep discount, and any hand that didn't contain at least three of them was considered pretty much dead on arrival. This was how it seemed to me anyway, as a dilettante, but then it was often hard to tell which of the cards in play was which because of the palimpsest of surreptitious markings, grease smears, and tobacco stains they had accumulated over the centuries. And what's more, with the help of the feeble light in the belowdecks, a man sequestering a well-masticated plug of tobacco in his cheek and a spot of larceny in his heart could use a strategically placed thumbprint permeated with dark juices to instantly convert a four into a five, a six into a seven, or, if he dared to use both thumbs at once, make a nearly useless ace into a valuable trey.

I played only occasionally at the poker coaxed from this singular deck, largely because its recondite and highly changeable rules were beyond me, and because I had nothing to wager except my pressure suit, which was more valuable to me than a sackful of gold. For the record, Bemis was a purist in these matters and would not touch the game.

He and I set about filling our air cylinders from the several hoses running up from Mister Lovelace's machines, and revitalizing our batteries with electrical energy from the same source. As we prepared for the vacuum, a few of the men stopped trying to modify the number of pips on their cards long enough to try to dissuade us from our mission.

"That's a bad spur, boys," said Watkins, whom I had credited with more sense. "Won't find anything but trouble in there."

"Yessir. Mighty unlucky," agreed Winters, a former whaler.

Bemis, filling an air cylinder, scoffed, "How can a hole in the ground be unlucky?"

"Cuz it's got the ghost of a jonah in it, ain't it?" said Chalk. He threw down his handful of dilapidated pasteboards and rose from the deck in order to enlighten us further. "If there's anything more unlucky th'n that then I'd like ta know about it."

Calvin was not in the market and let Chalk know it. "Come now, Chalk. What is it exactly that a ghost can do to you, rattle his chains and make you piss down the leg of your suit? That's already standard procedure, as far as I can tell." A few of the men laughed at this. All the haggises I'd ever worn offered a receptacle for liquid waste, but it was up to the wearer to hit the bullseye.

Chalk said, "I'm only lookin' out fer ya, ya unnerstands. I become kinda attached ta you two since Samuel had his mishap." He paused to launch a bolus of tobacco at the communal spittoon and, hitting the mark, continued. "Yer jonah, ya see, 's oft times as heinous a creature deceased as when he was alive, as his malval'nt—his evil spirit is set loose to do supernatural forms a mischief that weren't available ta him whilst still in the flesh. Why, there were a jonah in the old Hermione outta Gloucester, as I recall. She lost a brace a harpoons and a string a barrels on a spermaceti and nothin' to show for it, all on account a the jonah, ya see, an' the men was feelin' right perturbed, then one day he—the jonah that is—fell outta the mizzentop durin' a blow. I ain't sayin' he was he'ped to it, ya unnerstand, 'cept like I says some a the men was perturbed. Anyhow, he hit the quarterdeck hatch cover with a awful noise an' went straight on through all the way ta the bilge, or nearly so." Chalk shook his head. "Took three days ta die, he did, an' a moanin' somethin' horrible the whole time, but there weren't nothin' for it, as we di'n't have no proper surgeon aboard, only a loblolly boy, an'—he's dead now so's I don't mean no disrespect—he weren't quite right in the head, from the laudanum, I 'spect. But the jonah—I believe his name was Dutourd and so he were a frog a course, an' I leaves ta you what ta make a that."

I checked the gauge in front of me. I had filled an entire air cylinder and Chalk had barely finished killing off his jonah.

"Now I ain't sayin' all yer jonahs is of French extraction, mind you, fer the Devil don't make things that simple, do he? So—"

Bemis, now stripped to his under-drawers, said, "Is there an end to this tale?"

"So, as I was about ta tell ya," Chalk continued, "he dies—Dutourd that is, not the loblolly boy—an' once he's passed an' his remains gone over the side, well, shipmates, after that there weren't a moment's peace in the barky. Sure's yer born, not a dog watch'd go by where ya couldn't hear his incorporeal body hit the deck. Made a horrible noise, it did, again an' again, right about two bells, which was when he'd finally passed, ya see. It were a trial then, sleepin' through a night watch in the Hermione."

"It'd make for a better tale if it happened when he fell, rather than when he died," I said.

Chalk looked at me, albeit with pity more than scorn, and said, "Which he fell outta the mizzen top in the noon watch, di'n't he, an' no shade, not even the shade of a jonah, is about ta haunt a ship in the daylight. Even a lubber like yerself should know that much."

"I was only trying to help," I said, sliding my wounded leg carefully into the lower portion of my suit.

"You make fun all ya like, Samuel Clemens, but you'll be singin' a darker tune when the ghost a ol' Jonesy come outta that hole in D2."

Well now, I thought, this was some hard information for a change. "What hole is that?"

"Ah, there's a crack in the tunnel floor about a dozen feet to leeward—"

"Shipmate," I said, "I happen to know what leeward means, and it has no place in the Moon."

"The hole's there nonetheless," Chalk insisted. "An' when ol' Jonesy's shade comes breachin' up outta that hole like a spermaceti with a harpoon up its arse then you'll know better, won't ya now? An' that's a fact."

"And what will it do then?" Calvin said as he helped me get into the rest of my suit.

Chalk shook his head. "I know ya means well, Calvin Bemis, but yer a speakin' outta ign'rance, an' that's all I c'n say. I jus' pray that ign'rance don't git you an' Samuel, or all a us, dead. Why, ya could fall straight down that hole, couldn't ya, or did ya not think a that?" I expected I could fall into a hole on my own, without the help of a jonah, ghost or not.

"The hole the ghost comes out of?" Bemis said. "Sounds a bit crowded in there."

"You scoff all ya want, but I tell ya the man were a jonah, sure's yer born."

Perkins came into the belowdecks then and heard the fateful word.

"Shade or no, he'll always—"

"Stow it, ya silly booger," Perkins barked, and after a moment the old whaler returned, grumbling, to his hand of cards.

Seeing that Bemis and I were nearly ready for the vacuum, Perkins, who was already suited, plucked his helmet from the rack and led the way out of the belowdecks toward the airlock.

As we were leaving, Chalk mumbled, "An' whilst yer down there, you'll keep yer radios turned off, if ya knows what's good fer ya."

Chapter Seven

It was oddly satisfying to be back inside my dear haggis again, prowling through the cold pitch-black airless tunnels of the Deirdre mine. The sense of satisfaction was not particularly keen, and did not last much beyond the consumption of my first cylinder of air, but it confirmed for me that I was, for better or worse, a bonafide Moon rat.

As expected, Calvin and I were carrying a hod, and although we were heading down-tunnel into the D line, the hod was already full to the gunwales, in fact well above any real or imagined gunwales, with supplies and equipment to be employed in sinking the new shaft. And lying low amongst the innocent rope, shovels, spare batteries and air cylinders, our cargo included a cache of explosives. We had no concept of the volatility of these exceptional passengers—the box of brown cigar-like cylinders looked harmless enough—but we thought it best to assume that they were prepared to detonate themselves for as little as a stern glance or harsh word, and we handled the hod accordingly. This was not the case of course: it takes something more precise, such as a sudden burst of electricity, to set them off. We learned all about this soon enough, but not soon enough to keep us from carrying the hod like it was baby Jesus in the manger. Lang and Perkins led the way, and they got farther and farther ahead as we nursed our hod full of destruction into the depths of the Deirdre. I tried not to consider their increasing distance from us and our cargo as evidence of the likelihood of our imminent demise, but the farther ahead they got, the harder it was to maintain my complacence.

Eventually Mister Lang put an end to my uneasiness, or a reasonable portion of it, by backtracking far enough for his radio to be heard, and saying, "Clemens, is your leg troubling you?"

I thought this mighty solicitous, especially for a man with a reputation as something of a hard horse, and felt satisfied all over again. However, the leg was holding up quite well, the only sign of its ordeal being a tingling in the missing toe that was almost comforting by then, like a cryptic but reassuring message from a close relative now beyond this world.

I said, "No, thank you, Mister Lang. The leg is doing well."

"Then what the devil's keeping you men?" he said. "You get much farther behind and we'll lose you. Or are you satisfied that you can find your way to D2 by yourselves?"

This was indeed possible—but then so is a virgin birth, according to widely held opinion—it was just exceedingly unlikely.

"You'd best not count on that," I said. "We were only trying to—to be cautious."

Perkins, coming up behind Lang, could be heard over the radio snorting with derision. "They think the dynamite's gonna explode if they drop the hod, the boogers." That was not in fact the case. We, or at least I, strongly suspected that the cargo would explode if we disparaged its mother. We knew for a fact that it would explode if we dropped the hod.

"Move it along then," Lang said. "There's only so much air in the cylinders." So we did as he asked and picked up the pace, but still could not resist babying the hod over the rough patches.

Eventually we arrived at D2, which I had not visited before, or if I had I did not recognize any of its features—but then, despite the spur's elaborate reputation, there was little of note to see. I shone the beam of my headlamp around looking for a sign, such as Dante found at the gates of Hell perhaps, but there was only D2 scratched into the rock, so all hope was not abandoned, as yet. We carried the hod around and over a steep dogleg in the tunnel, and then came to a place where the passage was loaded with debris, presumably tailings that had yet to be hauled out to the surface. I presumed this, I should say. Calvin had another notion.

"Is this where the tunnel fell in?" he said, and added, "Where the man was killed?"

"That's right," said Lang peremptorily. "So mind your step."

Not far beyond this came another dogleg. These arbitrary twists and turns were ubiquitous in the Deirdre, and I had no idea why this should be. I assumed they were the result of a lack of skill or care during the excavation process, or simple cussedness and a desire to make life interesting for the men toting hod. I am always pleased to offer an opinion, and especially so on matters about which I am ignorant, since the field of play is so much broader that way. So in that spirit, or else simply to complain, I said, "Why, there's not a straight passageway in this entire enterprise, is there?"

"Not a one," said Perkins. He did not elaborate.

"Is there method to it then?" I wondered aloud. "I seem to recall something about a straight line being the shortest distance between two points, but perhaps that proposition is only valid on Earth." I thought this provocative enough to knock loose a response, if not an actual explanation, but once again I was wrong. It took Bemis to explain.

"The sharp turns serve to protect the miners from the blasts," he said. "Flying debris can't turn corners." So I was enlightened just in time to see the practice in action.

"This'll do," said Lang. "You men can drop the hod here."

We did not drop the hod, any more than we would have pitched the baby Jesus to the ground, but it arrived there eventually.

"Watch where you step," Perkins said. "There's a hole hereabouts big enough to fall into."

I swept my headlamp's beam around the floor of the tunnel and thought I saw what might have been a small crevasse, leading down and away from the tunnel itself. Lang and Perkins led us past this hazard and into a particularly narrow passage a few yards beyond. There they stopped. It was either that or turn back, because this was a dead end.

The two men then began a close inspection of the walls and floor of this small space. They poked and prodded at various concavities and protrusions of what looked to me very much like rock, then used a small pick to break off interesting pieces of it and held them in the glare of their headlamps.

"Here'll do," said Lang at last, pointing at an undistinguished patch of rock with the five sausages of his gloved right hand.

Perkins said, "Takes us mighty near the line, digging on that side."

"Captain says we're to proceed regardless," Lang replied. "Impossible to know for certain how far west we've dug." I had no idea what they were talking about, and I was not even sure the word *west* held any meaning in the Moon.

Lang then returned to the hod, presumably to decant the baby Jesus and his accoutrements for business, but Perkins remained behind and then beckoned to us, saying, "Look here, men." We looked, eager to see something engaging, such as a great bolus of water ice ripe for the picking. "You see there, those particles of white?"

"That's ice," claimed Bemis, who was always an optimist.

"Yes," Perkins affirmed.

"It's not much, is it?" I added. As I said, Calvin is the optimist.

"No, it ain't," Perkins agreed, perhaps a bit peevishly. "It's what's behind it, or below it, that we're after. If it's there." He used one of the sausages attached to his hand to prod the filaments of ice. "Not the strongest lead I've seen, not by a long shot, but you do what you can with what you have."

"Will we be blasting then?" I said, not sure if I wanted to witness the spectacle or not.

"That's how she's done, Clemens. About time you —"

"One of you men come lend me a hand," Lang said suddenly. Although one could often hear breathing and other sounds of human life through the radios, it was easy to forget that others could hear everything you said if they were close by.

Bemis went to help Mister Lang, and Perkins continued, "As I was saying, it's about time you boys lost your virginity." I chuckled, catching his meaning. "Your great digging leviathan notwithstanding, blasting and plenty of it is the way to mine the Moon."

This does not apply to strip mining, as done by the likes of Lunar Consolidated Mines, but then they are not after ice, or even precious metals, although those do turn up now and then in small quantities. No, the pigs graze on rock and dust. This fodder is reduced to its constituent atoms through the efforts of large resonance engines catholic in their tastes, and the atoms thereby obtained must be useful, especially the aluminum and the oxygen I expect, otherwise all the expense and commotion, the pigs and pickers and all the rest, wouldn't be worth the trouble. Ice however, and lumps of nickel and iron, and the marvelous carbonaceous chondrite, from which, I'm told, anything short of the Last Supper or good manners can be fashioned, rarely if ever lie on the surface where they can be consumed by a roving pig. For these valuable wonders, one must go deep, and for that, blasting into the planet's bowels with dynamite is the thing, and pretty much the only thing, that will get you to it.

Calvin and Mister Lang returned a moment later with the goods, and they, Perkins and Lang that is, began to put it to work. Bemis and I looked on with the same rapt attention one might pay to an experienced lion tamer preparing his tools before entering the cage, and knowing that you might be asked to wield the whip and chair at the next show.

They began by excavating a narrow hole in the rock face, into which, I presumed from its size, they would insert the cigar of explosives. Then Lang produced a small box, which had been a passenger in the hod, but one that I had ignored due to the presence of the dynamite. I saw the famous name of Mister Nobel on its lid. Lang opened the box and drew out a tiny cylinder with two wires hanging from one end.

"What's that?" I asked.

"Blasting cap," said Lang. Then he turned and inserted the end without the wires into one end of the cigar of dynamite.

"Can it explode?" I inquired.

Perkins laughed. "Can it explode, he asks. Yes, Clemens, that is its sole purpose in life. It is perhaps a more valuable invention than the dynamite itself, and has prevented many an accidental death, both here and on Earth. The job of the blasting cap is to detonate the dynamite," he added helpfully.

"I see," I said. "And what detonates the blasting cap? Or does it have a mind of its own in that regard?" And to think I had wasted my time caressing the mere dynamite, when my terror should have been saved for this unassuming device.

"No, no," Perkins said. "That's the whole point, you see. This fellow—" He held the dynamite in the beam of his headlamp. "—is made from nitroglycerine, which by itself is extremely volatile." Perkins waggled the deadly cigar about as if his place in Heaven had been bought and paid for in advance. "But thanks to the great Alfred Nobel, who thought to mix the nitroglycerine with diatomaceous earth and thereby render it harmless—" He tossed the supposedly harmless exploding cigar up into the vacuum, preparing to catch it once it had turned over and made its laborious descent, but it struck the ceiling of course, his sausage-shaped fingers fumbled the catch, and the dynamite fell to the ground. Before I had learned of the existence of diatomaceous earth, I would have ducked and thrown myself to the ground, in an altogether different direction, but enlightened as I now was, I only cringed a bit.

"Booger," muttered Perkins, then he bent and retrieved the dynamite, which I remembered too late also held the blasting cap. "See," he said, "entirely harmless."

"But," I said, "what about your blasting cap? Why didn't—"

"Yes," he continued, "Mighty ingenious, i'n't it?"

"I hope so," I said.

"It's made from fulminate of mercury, you see."

I didn't see.

"Once it's ignited, it'll set off your dynamite every time."

"And what angers the fulminate of mercury enough to set it off?" I asked.

"Electricity," he said triumphantly.

"I should have known," I said.

Calvin and I watched as Lang attached a pair of wires to those protruding from the blasting cap, and snugged the completed assembly into the hole they'd prepared in the rock. The wires were then strung backwards away from the rock face. I stood watching this until Mister Lang turned his lamp on me and said, "Come along now, unless you'd like to be exploded." This was not a part of my plans, so I followed on his heels, trying to stay as close to the twin air cylinders on his back as I could without knocking him over.

The four of us moved a fair distance from the dynamite, but, unlike everywhere else in the Deirdre, there was no dogleg close at hand around which we could hide from the blast—or to be more accurate, no dogleg within reach of the available length of wire. Had I been in charge I expect we would have got more wire, a lot more wire, then uncoiled it all the way back to the belowdecks, if not to Lucky Strike, but my opinion was not solicited in the matter.

Lang said, "We've only another few yards left on the spool. Any ideas, Lawrence?" this being Perkins's given name.

Perkins did not respond with his superior's Christian name, which was Percy, or perhaps Percival, but he did respond with an idea, and one I liked, which was no easy task under the circumstances. "You and the men go back out past the last bend in the tunnel. I'll go down into the hole here and set it off."

"Yes," Lang said after a moment, "the hole. I'd forgotten that. But let's see if the four of us can get into it. If so, it'll make for a good base of operations for subsequent blasts." I didn't like this plan nearly as well as Perkins's, but once again I wasn't asked for my opinion.

"Very well," Perkins said, then added, "In you go, boys, and bring the hod with you, or the supplies in any case."

Calvin went first, disappearing into the crevasse at our feet until only the shiny top of his helmet was visible in the light from my lamp.

"Hand down the air cylinders, Sam," he called. I did as instructed, then passed along the remaining contents of the hod, including the rest of the dynamite, which still received first class service, despite its lowered status in our eyes. We kindly let Mister Percy Lang keep charge of the box of blasting caps.

All the supplies having been shifted, I climbed down into the hole after them. It was not a lot snugger than the usual tunnel in the rest of the Deirdre, but it led nearly straight down, which meant that I had to take care not to step on Bemis on the way in. There were plenty of protruding points of rock to entertain us on the descent, and I noticed that more than one of them had a smear of the execrable grease, or slush as the whalers called it, on them. The odd thing was, Bemis didn't wear the slush, nor did any of the rest of us—but then, I thought, it could have been deposited back when D2 was a fresh spur with its whole life ahead of it.

Calvin was wedging the contents of the hod into niches and cracks in the sides of the crevasse with an admirable resourcefulness, and would soon have had everything neatly stowed if I had not inadvertently kicked him on the side of his helmet while trying to establish my footing. He lost his grip on the air cylinder he had been holding, and it fell between his feet and rattled on down into the craggy darkness below. I say it rattled just to be entertaining; in fact we heard no sound at all from its glancing descent.

"My apologies, Cal," I said. "I'll go on down and retrieve it."

"That's all right," he replied. "I'll fetch it," and he soon climbed down out of sight of my headlamp's penumbra.

With nothing else to do, I took what I assumed to be my station in the crevasse, bracing myself against the surrounding rock. I could hear the scraping of the air cylinders on my back as they found purchase on the wall behind me. This was a sound I had heard conducted through my haggis often enough while worming my way along the Deirdre's tunnels, but this time it gave me a renewed sense of the closeness of the space I was currently occupying. A previous blast, and one a fair distance away, had collapsed a portion of the tunnel above us. What if the charge we had set so close to hand collapsed the crevasse, or else discharged a shower of rock down into the already snug hole? Fortunately, Calvin stopped this unhappy train of thought by speaking to me out of the darkness below.

"Sam," he whispered, "will you come down here for a minute."

"I suppose, Calvin, but what can I possibly—"

"Just come, will you please, Sam."

His tone, although not revealing his intentions, brooked no argument. I pointed the beam of my helmet lamp downward so I could locate handholds and other protuberant hazards, then worked my way down to where my partner sat, resting on a narrow ledge that seemed to mark where the crevasse abruptly turned sideways and stretched away more or less horizontally into the rock.

"Well, here I am, Calvin. Now what is it that—"

"Shh—"

"But I—"

"Quiet, Sam. Just take a moment and listen."

I did as he asked, and for my trouble heard Mister Lang order Perkins into the hole above us. Then, once Lang had ceased speaking, I heard another sound.

"What's that?" I said.

"Shush, Sam"

I shushed, and listened intently, trying to resolve the sound coming through my radio into something I could recognize and comprehend. Straining to hear over the sounds of my own breathing and other telltale noises inside my suit, I at last made out an odd wavering noise that just might have been a human voice. It was tenuous and distorted, with static discharges rattling through it like gravel thrown into a miner's rock-washing trough. I continued listening, even holding my breath, and I could tell from its absence that Calvin was doing the same. And the longer I listened, the more certain I became that the sound I was hearing was indeed a human voice, and by my reckoning it appeared that its producer was not in the best of spirits. I could not make out a single word of what it said, so faint and distorted was the sound, but it seemed to me that the voice, or the owner of it anyway, was angry, sullen, demanding, forlorn, indignant, and distraught by turns. For some reason it did not occur to me that the voice I thought I heard could have belonged to more than one man.

I listened, and longed to understand what the eerie, distant, disembodied voice was saying, but still not a word was clear enough to be sure of its meaning. All that could be made out for certain was its dreadful, chilling tone.

Then I recalled Chalk, and the tale he had told.

"Holy God, Cal," I whispered. "It's Chalk's ghost."

Bemis made a derisive grunt. "It's something, anyway. I'll grant you that."

Then Perkins's voice came loud and clear over the radio. "Clemens. Bemis. Where the booger have you got to?"

"We're here," I said inanely. "You'll never guess what we've—"

"Shh," Calvin whispered, and he poked me with his boot for emphasis. "Not now."

"You two get up here where I can keep an eye on you," Perkins said. "We'll be blasting any minute now."

I scrambled up into the narrow passage above me until Perkins's boot landed a blow to my helmet.

"Ah, there you are. Pardon me, Clemens," he said.

"Think nothing of it," I replied. I was in a mood to be generous. After all, what was a simple kick to the head when compared to being stuck at the bottom of a crevasse in company with a ghost? And then there was the dynamite to consider, and the fulminate of mercury. "What happens now?" I said.

"Put out your helmet lamps," came Lang's voice. "They're no use in here."

Except perhaps to ward off the occasional ghost, I thought, but I did as he suggested. In my current frame of mind, the sight of the unyielding rock a hand's breadth from my faceplate was far too evocative of the grave.

It was Perkins, perched directly above me, who answered my question. "Now we attach the leads to a charged condenser and throw the switch."

"When?" I said.

Perkins laughed. "Whaddya mean when? Now."

Lang called out, "Fire in the hole."

"When will we know if it—" I began, then the rock all around me trembled, as if the planet had been stuck by a meteor. A loose pebble clattered off my helmet, but aside from that there wasn't a single sound to mark the occasion.

A minute later, we had our helmet lamps alight again, and were climbing out of the hole. Bemis began to hand up the supplies, but Lang said to leave them where they were for the moment, as more blasting was likely to be needed before we were through, and he was right.

Once we had returned to the belowdecks and removed ourselves from our pressure suits, I took Calvin aside. "Don't you think we should tell Mister Lang about what we heard?" I said. "Or Perkins anyway. He's a decent fellow."

He said, "And have them mock us for a pair of superstitious fools? No, thank you."

"We've been laughed at before, as I recall, and for sounder reasons."

The belowdecks was close and overcrowded, as always. Bemis glanced around at Chalk and the other men who had refused the assignment in D2 as they worked doggedly at their fantastical game of poker, then led me over to the vestibule containing the shaft leading down into Mister Lovelace's lair.

Taking me by the arm, he said intently, "We've got no proof, Sam. No evidence at all of what we heard. Nor can we say with any degree of certainty what it actually was."

"It has to be Chalk's ghost," I said. "The ghost of his jonah John Jones, that is, stalking the tunnels of the Deirdre in search of, I don't know, revenge, I suppose, or whatever it is that a ghost might desire."

Bemis looked at me with a contempt only slightly diluted by consternation. "I don't believe in ghosts," he insisted. "And unless I miss my guess, you don't either, Sam Clemens, despite the pleasure you take in playing the fool." He had me dead to rights, of course, but that didn't alter the facts.

"But what else could it be?" I insisted. "I haven't heard a voice so steeped in vitriol since I contrived to get a raccoon into bed with my old nanny." Calvin smiled in spite of himself. I added, "It was only a kit, but she was profoundly perturbed, so the critter had the desired effect."

He said, "I suppose I'd better check my hammock carefully with you about."

"No. I think you're safe from me, Calvin, at least for the time being. The pickings for such mischief are mighty slim hereabouts. One of Mister Kent's chickens might do, but I doubt it would sit still for the gaff, and Puss is far too proud to accept the role. But honestly, you heard that voice. Where could it have come from but beyond the grave?"

"So how was yer time down in the D2, shipmates?" This was Chalk of course, and he had snuck up behind us.

"Fine," Bemis said.

"Don't s'pose ya found any ice."

"We blasted three times," Calvin said. I noticed a tinge of aggravation in his tone. "Nothing much as yet."

"Well, leastways you's back in one piece. That's about as good as ya c'n e'spect, considerin'. Now, c'n I borrow yer sewin' needle then, Samuel Clemens? I bent the tip a mine probin' at a tooth, an' now she's broke clean off."

"Of course," I said. "Happy to, but I think it may still be in the sickbay."

"I'll be checkin' wi' Mister Kent then," he said, then added with a twinkle in his eye, "I 'spect you heard the voices."

Neither of us spoke.

"Thought as much," he said. There was a hint of triumph on his weather and tattoo ravaged face. "Wouldn't go back down there, I was you."

"I told you, Chalk," Bemis said. "I don't believe in ghosts."

Chalk turned away, saying, "Ghost don' care a lick if ya believes or not, Calvin Bemis, an' that's a fact." He glanced at me then. "I don' s'pose you'll mind if I keeps the needle then, Samuel." I looked at him without comprehension. "Once yer dead, that is," he said, then turned and shuffled off toward the galley.

Chapter Eight

The next course of dynamite gouged out a deep hole in the floor of D2, and once the dust had settled, which didn't take long, Perkins climbed into it to inspect the wreckage for signs of ice. I looked on with a good deal of anticipation, tempered somewhat by previous disappointments. I had been working in the Deirdre mine for several months by then, and had yet to see a nugget of ice much bigger than my fist, and I was with child, as the saying goes, to be witness to a big strike.

Perkins reached up and threw a shovel-full of blasted rock onto the ground at Mister Lang's feet. Lang picked some shards of rock out of the pile and gave them a brief examination in the beam of his headlamp. Then he tossed the shards aside and said, "So what do you think, Mister Perkins?"

Perkins's helmet lamp peeked over the edge of the rubble and lit up the floor of the cavern as he lifted another scoop of freshly blasted rock from the hole. "Well, I don't know," he began. "I expect you're a better judge of ore than I am, Mister Lang."

Lang snorted. "Don't be shy, Lawrence. What's your honest assessment?"

Perkins stood silently for a while, then at last he sighed and said, "There's booger all, Percy, that's what there is." And so it looked as if I would have to wait a while longer to see that big strike.

"I'm afraid I have to agree," Lang said, then added solemnly, "Captain isn't gonna like it much."

"No. I expect he ain't," agreed Perkins. "Well, shall I have the men—" by which he meant Bemis and me of course, "—collect this up and take it topside?"

"Not worth the hauling," said Lang, with evident disdain, then after half a minute of silent contemplation, added, "But then we've got to give it every chance, don't we, Mister Perkins. Let me have a closer look." He grabbed Perkins by the bloated arm of his haggis and, taking unthinking advantage of the meager gravity, hoisted him effortlessly out of the six-foot deep hole. Then he jumped down and began to examine more pieces of rock, which he then tossed out of the pit with a casual indifference that did not speak well for their quality.

Bemis and I stood by with nothing in particular to do. Despite several worthy explosions that produced plenty of destruction, we had found no ice ore of sufficient quality to be escorted out of the depths, and we were not sent down into the great crack in the floor either. A new, far lengthier skein of electrical wire had been obtained from stores, so instead of descending into the crevasse for protection, we retreated around the final dogleg of D2 to hide from the blasts.

I approved of this arrangement on several counts. Although the procedure amounted to lying flat on the ground and waiting for it to shake apart beneath you, it was easily more comfortable and convenient than climbing down into a crevasse, and by my reckoning just had to be safer—unless of course the roof fell in on top of us, as it had on the ill-fated John Jones. The new procedure also prevented me from listening to the ghost, since there wasn't a trace of its anguished vocalizations up in the D2 itself. It seemed that the vituperous, if otherwise unintelligible, creature only deigned to speak to Bemis and myself, and then only when we were at the bottom of the crevasse.

After another few minutes spent chucking rocks out of the new hole, Lang said, "Lawrence, prepare another stick. I think we'll give it one more try. There's a weak area here that should give way and open up a new pocket underneath."

"Aye-aye," said Perkins. Then he turned to me. "Clemens, get out a stick of dynamite and a blasting cap. You know where they are." Indeed I did. They were back around the last dogleg, resting in the hod. I went to retrieve the goods requested, and returned with them to where Perkins stood beside the pit. I made as if to hand him the dynamite and the blasting cap, but he did not take them. Instead he said, "You prepare it, Clemens. It's simple enough."

I opened a hole in the wrapping surrounding the deadly cigar, then carefully inserted the business end of the cap, making sure it was fitted securely in place.

"Shall I attach the wires?" I asked. I had watched them do this enough times that I felt reasonably confident in my ability to carry out this procedure as well. Perkins agreed and I retrieved the spool of wire and the boning knife we used to strip the resinous cloth insulation from its ends. It is not an easy task to scrape wires clean of their coverings when your fingers are encased in ten thick sausages, but I eventually managed it. Then I twisted the wires I'd uncovered together with those from the blasting cap, making sure, as Perkins had shown me, not to tangle them together and, as they say in the electrical trade, "short them out."

At last satisfied, I handed the assemblage over to Perkins. He took it carefully in his own collection of sausages, inspected it briefly, then passed it on to Mister Lang at the bottom of the hole. A minute later, Lang climbed out and we all retreated back around the dogleg, with Bemis and Perkins uncoiling the wire from its spool as they went. Soon we were all flat on the ground, Mister Lang spoke the ritual incantation "fire in the hole," and once again the ground shook beneath us.

Then, even before the shaking had entirely subsided, a distorted eruption of oaths and wailing spilled out of my radio's speaker. I raised my helmeted head and looked around to see which of us had been injured by the blast. Perhaps rock fragments had learned to travel around corners after all, I thought. But my three companions all appeared to be unhurt.

The cry came again, and although it was ripe with anguish, it was not a cry born of pain, or not physical pain in any case, but of rage.

"Good God," I said, "we've unleashed the ghost!" This eventuality should have caused me to turn and run, and not stop running until I'd reached New Orleans, but instead a mad curiosity overcame me. Unthinking, I leapt to my feet and ran the wrong way —that is, into the dogleg. And as my reward for this madness, when I rounded the corner my headlamp's beam indeed revealed a strange and monstrous apparition. A lumpy sphere, something like the helmet of a pressure suit, seemed to rise by itself out of the ground and float in the vacuum.

"Calvin," I shouted, "come quickly! You're not gonna believe this." Meanwhile the sphere continued to ascend, and soon what looked to be a pressure suit emerged below it. It was not an ordinary suit, however, but one strangely appropriate to a ghost or a ghoul, for it was painted or tarred to a pitch black, and would have been completely invisible were it not for the gleam of its metal fittings reflecting in the beam from my lamp.

I felt a touch on my haggis and looked back to see that Bemis, and Perkins and Lang as well, had come around the dogleg and were standing beside me.

"Booger me," said Perkins.

This was well spoken, considering the circumstances, but it was the ghost who had the floor, and it used it, shouting, "Now you'll pay for what you done, ya rotten barstards. Just see if you don't." The voice was unmistakable. I recognized it immediately. Here was the source of the tortured cries I'd heard at the bottom of the crevasse. This was Chalk's ghost, sure's yer born, as Chalk himself would no doubt say.

Then I saw something that amazed me more than seeing Chalk's ghost in the flesh, if that is possible. As I watched, and listened to the ravings of the primary apparition, another man, or ghoul, or animated pressure suit in any case, came up out of the ground, and behind that came another, and a moment later yet another emerged out of the deep pit that was the result of our recent blasts.

Then the ghost said, "Which a you sons-a-bitches is Merriwether?"

"What?" said Mister Lang.

"You heard me. Which a you barstards is the tyrant Merriwether?"

One of the others who had emerged from the hole said, "Don't matter, Johnny. They's all a them fuckin' Deirdres."

"Shut up!" barked the ghost named Johnny, who it seemed was not much of a ghost after all.

"Who are you men?" Mister Lang said. "Where did you come from?"

Perkins spoke then, saying, "Good Lord, Percy, I know that voice. It's Jones. He's—"

"Jones is dead," said Lang, incorrectly, as it turns out.

"Which one?" screamed the ex-apparition Jones.

Lang said, "The captain's up top supervising the loading of the next ore shipment."

"Course he is," said Jones, sounding oddly pleased. "No dirty work for him, no sir. No diggin', no blastin', no toting hod all the day long. No taking abuse from ign'r'nt whaler scum like Winters and that goddamn Gottschalk. No sea trash callin' ya jonah just cuz they'd broke their own damned leg. No roof fallin' in ta crush the life outta ya. Nooo. Not fer the likes a him, the great Captain Merriwether. Now ain't that a laugh." Jones tried to laugh here, but failed. "Captain is he? I say slaver's more like it. An' captain a what, I ask you? Captain of a hole in the ground, that's what. Captain of a fuckin' great hole in the ground. Him and his nasty little butt boy Lang. Now there's a right barstard deserves to die a slow death, like he done for me." He paused for breath, then snarled, "Which one a you's Lang then?"

"That would be me," Mister Lang said, and he raised an arm to indicate which of the anonymous haggises he was encased in. "What do you men want?" he added.

"Plenty," said Jones.

One of the men who'd come up out of the ground said, "Don' play at no dog in the manger. You maggots is jumpin' our claim."

The four of us stood frozen in place, stunned into immobility by a perfect bewilderment. Mister Lang's question had been a good one: Aside from the jonah and ex-apparition Jones, who were these men? And how had they got here? Well, I knew how to answer the second question at least. Jones had come up out of the crevasse, but the others had climbed into D2 through the hole we had just now blasted open for them.

"We want plenty," Jones repeated. "We'll have it all before we're through. But," he continued, "Mister Lang, first I believe I'll have you dead. Like you done for me." Neither one of them appeared to be dead so far, I noticed. Then again, that could change in a hurry. John Jones had produced a pistol in one sausage-fingered hand. It ran through my mind that it would be a tricky business to pull the trigger with a sausage for a finger, when suddenly there was a brilliant flash, and Mister Lang gave a startled cry. I looked in his direction and saw an awful, great, fulminating geyser of air explode from the thigh of his pressure suit.

"That'll do, I reckon. Oughta take a good long time. Now who're you?" Jones barked again. And to my horror he turned his haggis, and the pistol, toward me. "That filthy little gnome Gottschalk I 'spect. Least I hope so."

"N-no," I croaked. It was all I could manage under the circumstance, and indeed it was not enough.

"Well you're a shit-crawlin' worm of a Deirdre an' that makes ya ripe for the killin'." Seeing what had happened to Mister Lang, I wasted no time in diving for the ground, but as I went down I saw Bemis pick up a rock—there were plenty to hand after all—and throw it hard at the collection of sausages holding the pistol. It went true and struck Jones's arm with enough force to send the weapon flying into the dark.

"Bravo, Calvin," I cheered. This was neither the first nor the last time that Calvin Bemis saved my life, but it is about my favorite of the lot, I think.

Meanwhile, Perkins had hauled Mister Lang to his feet and carried him back around the corner of the dogleg behind us. Jones was stunned by the impact of Bemis's throw, but not much damaged by it, unfortunately. He raised his arms and began to come towards the remaining two of us, imitating the monstrous apparition he in his heart was.

"Let's move," Calvin said, and he picked up another rock and hurled it at the approaching black haggis. I finally got the message and began throwing stones myself. Most missed the mark, but one—it was another of Calvin's I suspect—struck Jones on the side of his helmet and caused him to stagger back. We took this opportunity to duck around the dogleg to momentary safety.

Mister Lang's badly deflated pressure suit was lying on the ground, and Perkins knelt beside it, pinching closed the hole in its thigh, but with only partial success, if the spurts of precious vapor that escaped around the sausages were any indication.

"Clemens, get a patch and the tin of sticking tar out of the hod. Mister Lang may or may not survive the wound, but he'll not decompress on my watch." I located the hod and soon found the patching kit. You can be sure that since I'd lost that toe to a leaking pressure suit, I was always conscious of the whereabouts of the patching kit, although it had done me no good at the time.

"Who are those men?" asked Bemis. "I gather that the lunatic in the tarred suit is John Jones, but who're —"

"Whoever they are," I interrupted, squatting beside Lang and opening the kit, "they'll be comin' 'round the mountain any second."

Perkins said, "The two of you will have to hold them off while I tend to Mister Lang."

"We'll try," I said, rising to my feet and then scanning the ground around me for a batch of throwable stones.

The doglegged passage was less than a dozen yards long, and narrow enough, as most such passages in the Deirdre were, so that only a single man in a pressure suit could negotiate it at any one time. Bemis was already standing athwart the passage with a rock in each hand. I looked into the blackness where I thought the tunnel might be and saw the flare of a helmet lamp as a man came around the bend. I saw Bemis's arm shoot out and a rock passed through the beam of my headlamp. At the same instant I caught the glint of metal in the suited man's glove. Jones, or someone, had retrieved the gun.

I shouted, "Calvin!" then shoved him to the ground just as a flash erupted out of the darkness. "He's found the pistol."

Bemis sat up and wasted no time in hurling another stone into the passage. That one must have connected with something, since it drew a spate of oaths from our assailant. Then he growled, "It's the men of the Hammer 'n' Tongs come ta get theirs, ya thieving pirates. I warned 'em long ago you'd be comin' ta steal their rightful claim, and lo an' behold here ya are, jus' like I said." There was another silent flash as Jones again fired the pistol. They are disconcertingly quiet, these gun fights on the Moon. Living on Earth, a man comes to expect a considerable noise to accompany each discharge, but out here a firing squad could be hard at work directly behind you, and you wouldn't notice a thing until you were dead.

"Turn out your lamps," shouted Perkins. "You're making yourselves an easy target." We did as he instructed, and as an enthusiastic coward, I felt foolish not to have thought of this myself. We returned then to throwing rocks at our assailant. After a moment there came a startled cry over the radio, and the light in the passage disappeared. From this I concluded that Bemis, or by some miracle I, had at last managed to acquaint Mister Jones with another rock.

"I think I got his headlamp," Calvin said. Then added, "I don't suppose we have a pistol of our own."

"Cap'n has a brace," came the ragged voice of Mister Lang. I realized I'd been hearing his heavy, labored breathing for the last few minutes. "In his cabin."

"No good to us there," said Bemis.

"Mister Lang is badly wounded," announced Perkins then. "I've patched the hole in his suit but he's bleeding out, sure's yer—" He began again. "We have to get him to Mister Kent as soon as possible." The unspoken words, *or he'll die*, hung ominously in the vacuum.

Lang croaked, "We're outnumbered, I expect, and completely outgunned. Take the men and get out, Lawrence. 's no use us all dying down here."

"Booger that," said Perkins. "You men put Mister Lang in the hod—leave everything out but the dynamite, can't let them get their hands on that—then start carrying him up the D line fast as you can go. I'll bring up the rear and keep them off as long as I can."

Lang cried out through clenched teeth as we laid him in the hod, but otherwise did not protest, and we were soon lurching awkwardly over the fallen debris that had most assuredly, we knew now, not killed the jonah John Jones, and out of the (now fully confirmed as unlucky, even if not haunted) D2.

I glanced back from my now especially coveted place at the front of the hod and saw Perkins coming along behind us, hopping sideways like a pressure-suited crab, cradling an armload of rocks and hurling one occasionally into the tunnel behind him.

"Face forward, Sam," whispered Bemis, although whispering was pointless to my way of thinking. "Don't give them a target." I, being in the van, was allowed the use of my headlamp, which was also starting to dim, just to make matters more interesting. I turned back to my work and saw, once we had come around another of the ubiquitous doglegs I now cherished and adored, that we were about to ascend a steep and particularly narrow section of the D line.

"Hoist him up, Cal," I said. "It's about to get steep ahead." Then, to our passenger, I said, "Mister Lang, keep your arms and legs drawn in if you're able."

"'Don't bother," said Calvin. "He's unconscious."

Without thinking, I turned my head to look at Lang. "Lord," I began, "is he still—" There was a blinding flash that briefly silhouetted Perkins, and simultaneously fragments of rock exploded from the wall beside Bemis's head.

"Sam!" my partner shouted.

"Sorry," I said, resolutely facing forward again.

"Is he still breathing?" I asked, meaning Mister Lang of course. There was a part of me, one which I was not proud of, mind you, but still attentive to, that wished, in the kindest possible terms, that Lang had expired. There was no question we could escape a lot faster without the awkward burden of the hod.

"Yes, for the moment," Calvin reported. "At least I think so."

I was heartily glad to know this. I'd heard my conscience going over its notes, preparing to berate me in perpetuity for that one immoral thought.

I hoisted up my end of the hod and worked my haggis through the almost vertical stretch of tunnel. And then the hod, with its outsized and awkwardly shaped burden, ground to a stop behind me.

"It's stuck," said Bemis matter-of-factly.

"Can't be stuck," said Perkins. "They'll be on us in seconds if we don't keep moving." It's at times like these, I thought, that a conscience becomes particularly inconvenient.

"Leave the hod," said Perkins.

"What?" said Bemis. "We can't—"

"Pull Mister Lang out of the hod and leave it behind," he explained, much to the relief of my conscience.

Calvin and I wrestled the unconscious Lang from the hod, fortunately thinking to get him in front of it as we did so. Then Bemis and I proceeded to work his haggis (which, thanks to Perkins's efforts, was nearly as bloated as it should be once again) up through the narrow passage. My headlamp was necessarily pointed rearwards while I struggled to negotiate Mister Lang, and I saw, before Calvin blocked my view down the tunnel, that Perkins had somehow got himself in front of the hod, and was busy wedging its extremities as tightly as possible into the walls of the tunnel, leaving it thoroughly impassable, at least for the time being. Bemis and I had performed this feat by accident numerous times, and now I knew what the stunt could be good for.

We were obliged to carry Mister Lang from there on, as the hod was lost to us, albeit in a good cause. We could hear cursing over the radios as our pursuers, apparently the men of the Hammer 'n' Tongs in league with the madman Jones, fought to remove the obstruction from their path. Perkins must have done a fine job of positioning the hod, as the cursing was prodigious and grew ever fainter behind us.

Thanks to the weak gravity, Lang was not heavy, but his suit, with the twin air cylinders on its back, was tremendously awkward in the tight space. If Lang had been a sack of ore, or a congressman, we would have dragged him, but this was certain to rupture his suit if kept up for any length of time, so we had no choice but to carry him between us. The fact that he did not cry out, awaken, or even much stir under the necessarily rough treatment was a blessing for all of us, assuming of course that Lang would ever regain consciousness again.

Chapter Nine

Mister Lang, his blood-drenched body relieved of both pressure suit and under-drawers, lay atop a makeshift pallet assembled from sacks of flour and potatoes (the same ones, less a peck, that I had occupied after my own misadventure). He was deathly pale and for the moment unconscious, thanks to a prodigious dose of laudanum. I had been offered the bed of potatoes, but alas not the laudanum, as Mister Kent had not thought my agony momentous enough to require its services, prescribing an ocean of expensive whiskey instead. After all, from his perspective, it didn't hurt a bit.

"Will he live?" asked Captain Merriwether, gazing down with obvious affection at his first mate.

"That remains to be seen," said Kent, who was still busy bandaging the wound in Lang's thigh. Merriwether looked sharply at the Deirdre's physician, and Kent modified his assessment accordingly. "The bullet did not penetrate the femoral artery, or he would have been dead long before now. Still, he has lost a great deal of blood." He finished dressing the wound by wrapping a wide cloth bandage around the upper portion of Lang's thigh. "There is a good chance that he will recover, now that the bullet is out and the bleeding is stopped, but he'll not be able to walk for some considerable time, lest the wound open itself again. By all that's right, he should not even be moved for some days, but from what you've told me of our situation, we may have no choice."

"If they penetrate to the galley then we will have been defeated in any case," said Merriwether.

We had managed the rest of the trip back to the belowdecks and into the sickbay without further incident, but there was little doubt that an attack on the Deirdre, and perhaps even a full-scale invasion, was underway: an assault led by an apparent madman who, as I knew all too well, would not hesitate to shoot on sight anyone even remotely associated with the Deirdre.

To their credit, once they were apprised of the situation, the former whalers and other idlers camped in the belowdecks threw down their dilapidated aces, donned their pressure suits, and took up arms, of a sort, charging down into the D line wielding picks, shovels, and short lengths of aluminum and copper pipe. There only six defenders that I could count, and that number included Perkins and Calvin Bemis—in fact everyone except Mister Kent, Mister Lovelace, Mister Lang (for obvious reasons), the captain (at least for the moment), and myself. I had been granted a temporary deferment from this duty, ostensibly to act as a runner, communicating the captain's commands to Perkins and the others—

assuming I could find them in the rabbit warren that was the Deirdre, and especially the D line. I tried to tell myself that I had been chosen for this task because of my demonstrably superior rhetorical skills, but I suspected that the real reason was that I was considered the least useful man in a pipe and shovel fight.

As he secured Lang's bandage, Mister Kent said, "I don't understand, Eustace—why are they doing this?"

Captain Merriwether replied, "They think we're trying to poach on their territory—the Hammer 'n' Tongs's territory, that is. In the parlance of the prospecting trade, they believe we have jumped their claim. Then again, that doesn't account for the presence, let alone the behavior, of Mister Jones," he added.

"Well, that's nonsense, surely," Kent said. "We haven't trespassed on their mine."

The captain of the Deirdre was silent for an unnaturally long time. "Not necessarily," he said at last. "I'll admit we were sailing pretty close to the wind, reopening D2. It *is* hard by the Hammer 'n' Tongs, as far as it's possible to determine such things inside the Moon. It's possible we may have crossed the line." He paused again, then said, "Hell, Kent, I'll confess it, given what Perkins told me of the excavations there, it seems likely that we did blast a hole or two into their claim." He sighed. "What can I say, gentlemen? I plead desperation. And yes, before you say anything, I know full well that that is a poor excuse." He took a moment to look at Mister Lang, lying unconscious beside him, then shifted himself on the small barrel he was using as a stool. "It's a tolerably severe breach of etiquette, jumping a man's claim, even if done inadvertently, and I can understand why they might be upset over it. But that's no reason to board the Deirdre with guns blazing." He abruptly stopped speaking and leapt to his feet. "Oh my lord," he cried, "I've forgotten the pistols!" and he bolted from the sickbay-cum-galley without another word.

"Mister Lang did say the captain had a brace of pistols in his cabin," I explained.

Kent nodded, then said, "So we have jumped their claim, have we, and now they are after jumping ours." He shook his head. "Turnabout is fair play, I suppose, if it comes to that. But then who is this madman in the blackened pressure suit, this Jones, I believe you called him? Is he the owner of the Hammer and Tongs?"

I looked at Kent in astonishment. "You mean to say you don't know him?" I said.

He said, "Why no, Clemens. Should I?"

"Well yes," I said. "He was here. That is to say, he was a Deirdre once upon a time, if Chalk and the rest can be believed."

Mister Kent chuckled. "They're good men, Clemens, by and large, but I'd not rely much on anything they might say." Kent thought a moment, idly twisting the locks of his voluptuous beard. "Jones, is it? I believe there was a man by that name— could hardly fail to be so, sooner or later, considering it's so commonplace." He frowned, then said, "Why, he's not the man who was killed, is he?" Then he laughed. "I suppose that can hardly be the one, can it."

"As a matter of fact it is," I said, briefly enjoying the miracle of knowing something, anything, that someone else in my general vicinity did not. "It seems that the news of his death was greatly exaggerated," I concluded.

"Excuse me?"

"I mean to say that he was not killed after all, although I'm sure I don't know why not. It would have saved everyone involved a great deal of trouble, including him." This was harsh sentencing, I'll confess, but the man had shot at me with a pistol— done it more than once in fact, and without our even being properly introduced.

Kent said, "I knew him hardly at all, I'm afraid. He was never sick or injured that I can remember. That's how I get to know the men, you understand. Unless of course they make a habit of complaining about the grub."

"That was his great mistake," I said.

Kent looked at me quizzically.

"He remained healthy and uninjured while, at least to hear Chalk tell it, everyone else fell into rack and ruin around him. That made him a jonah, you see."

"Yes, I remember now. The men used to complain of him to me on occasion, but I paid it no mind. Nor did the captain, as I recall." He went back to twisting at his great beard. "And if I'm thinking of the right man, Mister Lang didn't care for him much and rode him hard. Or perhaps he did so to placate the other men, which is surely a bad business. I should have been more attentive to the men's conversation, I suppose, but then they're always going on about something, especially that Gottschalk." He took a moment to inspect Mister Lang, then said, "But still, he was trapped in a cave-in and never recovered, yes? I don't see how the man i'n't dead."

I heard a commotion and we both turned to see Captain Merriwether fly into the sickbay, looking like a desperado now with a six-gun clutched in each hand.

"Clemens," he barked, "you come with me. A pair of pistols should help even the fight."

I reached vaguely for one of the six-guns.

He saw my gesture and said, "Can you hit anything, man?"

I said, "I believe I could hit a rabbit with a rifle—if I was allowed to swing the butt at its head."

Merriwether did not laugh of course, but he didn't shoot me over the jest either, so I figured it had gone down reasonably well.

Then to my astonishment, as we left the sickbay for the belowdecks he pressed one of the pistols into my hand.

"Honestly," I began, "I'm not much of a—"

He said, "I want you to go back to the D line and find Perkins. He'll know what to do with this."

"All right," I said. I took the pistol carefully. It wasn't the baby Jesus, but it was holy enough.

"Mister Lang is the best shot among us, unfortunately," Merriwether added, glancing back toward the sickbay. "He having been in the army for a spell before he went to sea. But Perkins'll do."

Once we were in our pressure suits and into the tunnels, Captain Merriwether promptly disappeared, and I made my way to the start of the D line, which was an antechamber equipped with stray tailings, broken pieces of hod, and a two-foot-tall D scratched into the wall next to the entrance into the main passage. The D line was the largest and most extensive of the four excavations that made up the Deirdre, and was the most productive of the four as well, or had been at one time anyway. It was considerably less productive at present, if the results of our recent foray into D2 meant anything.

Two men were standing outside the D line when I arrived, pistol in hand. (By the way, there are no pockets to speak of in your typical pressure suit. I gather they tend to become impassable once the suit has ballooned up with air.)

"Who's that?" called one of the anonymous haggises, once I'd negotiated the inevitable dogleg and come into their view. (There are no identification marks on your typical pressure suit either.)

"Clemens," I said matter-of-factly.

"Ah, Samuel," said an unmistakable voice. "And ya brought me a pistol into the bargain."

I said, "I'm sorry, Chalk, but the captain says I'm to give this to Mister Perkins. Do you know where he is?"

It turned out that the other man was Winters. Like Chalk, he was a former whaler, and seeing the two of them there, staying scrupulously outside of the Ds, I wondered if somehow they still harbored a superstitious fear of the ghost of D2, despite the fact that the shade in question had proven itself to be mere flesh and blood.

Chalk said, "He's gone down to the D3," which I knew was actually above D2, although it was a later dig. "Leastways that's where he said he were goin'."

"He deputized us to guard the sally port," said Winters, raising a pickaxe to show that he was on the job.

I entered said sally port and started into the dreaded Ds. Officially, there were three excavations beyond the entrance to this line, called (with the sort of wild imagination common in the mining trade) D1, D2, and D3, but once you were inside, you soon discovered there were far more than three tunnels in it. This was so, I found out eventually, because whenever evidence of a fresh ice deposit was detected, whether that evidence was real or only hypothetical, blasting inevitably occurred and, human nature being what it is, more blasting soon followed, until a pocket of ice or other valuables was uncovered, or until (far more often, alas) it was given up as a "dry hole." Either way, a new spur was created, and every one of these once-promising boondoggles looked alike. Most of the spurs were dead ends, but now and then, just to make navigation more interesting, they would take it upon themselves to collide with others of their kind, appearing without warning anywhere above, below, or to either side of the tunnel you were currently in. The choice this provided gave some solace to a lost miner, because there was always a chance that the new tunnel might be a way out. Then again, it was at least as likely to lead you in circles, or to be another dead end, and at such a juncture it was useful to invoke the devil-may-care go-for-broke spirit of a busted-out riverboat gambler if you were not to go mad.

I had learned a fair portion of the D line by then, largely by the accumulation of mistakes. Thus I was able to find my way to D3 without much trouble. And once I'd got there, it was not necessary to guess which spur Perkins might be inhabiting, because he nearly ran me down by coming out of one in a hurry.

"Who's that?" he shouted. (I suppose name plaques are out of the question, but honestly, something should be done.)

"It's Clemens," I said.

A moment later, two more men came running out of the tunnel, one of whom I recognized as Calvin Bemis. (Pressure suits are not entirely anonymous after all, and considering our close acquaintance, I'd seen more of Bemis's mottled haggis than I'd seen of my own.)

There was a flash deep in the spur they'd just run out of, and a telltale geyser of dust and rock fragments sprang up from the floor of the tunnel's mouth. All four of us moved up the main passage to get out of the line of fire. Now I knew why they were so anxious to leave that spur.

"They've broken out of D2 and into D3 somehow," said Perkins, breathing hard into his radio's speaking cone. "And they have another pistol. Either that, or the one gets around quite a lot."

"I don't know if it'll help, but I've brought you this," I said, raising the captain's pistol into the beam of his headlamp.

"About damned time," said the other man, the one who wasn't Bemis.

"Booger all," Perkins said. "Will you look at that. Now we have a fighting chance at least." Perkins's faceplate pointed at me, and he said, "I don't suppose you're a crack shot then, are you, Clemens?"

I'd been around this track once already and didn't feel the need to run it again. "I'm afraid not," I said.

Perkins wasted no time in taking the six-gun from my glove. "Very well," he said. "Gather up your weapons, turn out your helmet lamps, and let's see if we can run them out of here." In addition to the pistol, our arsenal contained a shovel, a four-foot length of pipe, and all the rocks I could carry.

We put out our headlamps, and a moment later, in total darkness, Perkins leapt into the tunnel's mouth, firing the pistol once, then again a second later. A very satisfying series of exclamations came over the radio in response. I was about to tell him to go easy with the pistol, as Captain Merriwether had neglected to give me any ammunition beyond what was in the gun to begin with, but hearing that distant cursing reminded me that our adversaries were almost certainly able to hear us, and under no circumstances should they be informed about our short supply of bullets.

Then Perkins, knowing full well that we could see nothing at all, grabbed each of us in turn and drew us into the spur behind him until we reached the first dogleg. This feature was discovered the hard way, by running into the wall. The invaders were not there, thank goodness, but they were not far away. Distorted bits of chatter came over the radio, most of it commenting unfavorably on the presence of the new pistol.

The radios we use on the Moon are not designed for privacy, let alone the secrecy necessary to waging war. Quite the opposite in fact: all the radios operate on a common frequency, like steam buggies all traveling on the same turnpike. And so there was no way for us to talk amongst ourselves without the men of the Hammer 'n' Tongs on the far side of the dogleg hearing much, if not all, of what we said. Our only recourse was to shut off our radios entirely and communicate by touching our helmets together, thereby conducting the vibrations of our words through a combination of metal and air.

In my experience, an American finding himself in a foreign land communicates with the locals either through pantomime and wild emphatic gestures, like an Italian ordering his breakfast, or else by speaking his English slowly, distinctly, and as loudly as possible—hoping, one can only suppose, to penetrate the thick skull of the foreigner through brute force, like a cannon ball crashing through the hull of a man-o'-war. Neither of these techniques work any better in the tunnels of the Moon than they do in, say, Moldavia, but for even better reasons: hand gestures are unintelligible in total darkness, and no volume of sound, no matter how painfully enunciated, will ever penetrate the vacuum.

Perkins said, "Radios off. Then touch helmets."

So we switched off, and the four of us got straight to work banging our heads together. After he'd had enough of this, Perkins took charge and put Bemis on one side of him, up-tunnel, and me on his down-tunnel side, with the other man, who it turned out was Garrett, squeezed into the wall in front of him. Then each of us placed his helmet against that of Perkins.

"Can you men hear me?" Perkins said, but the problem was not so much hearing him as understanding him. The sound of his voice was thin and hollow, distant yet booming at the same time, as if he were speaking with his head thrust inside a large spittoon—which was within spitting distance of the truth. Still, noises of assent were delivered by the rest of us, and Perkins continued, "I think they're waiting for us just past the bend, figuring to jump us as we come through. So here's what we'll do—"

"Unless they've gone off down-tunnel," said Garrett. I think that is what he said. His voice was even more hollow and indistinct than Perkins's, as his spittoon was once removed from mine.

"If that's so, then we'll go after them, but I think they're waiting for us to come through one at a time so they can bushwhack us." As usual, the tunnel ahead was only wide enough for one fully-loaded haggis at a time to pass.

I said, "Mister Perkins, I think you should know that the captain did not give me any more ammunition for that six-gun."

"Booger," said Perkins, "and I just wasted two of them. And they've got smart and shut their lamps off."

"How do you know that?" I interrupted.

Bemis said, "Let's hear the plan, Sam."

Perkins answered my question anyway. "If they had a lamp on, we'd see some light spilling down the tunnel, despite the bend. So," he continued, "instead of charging in, I say we sneak up on them."

"We do what on them?" said Garrett.

"*Sneak up* on them," repeated Perkins, speaking more distinctly. "We can't go through except one-by-one, which is what they're counting on. So instead we go around, or two of us do, while the other two stay here, lamps off but radios on."

"What do you mean, go around?" said Bemis.

Perkins said, "You've got to know your D line, you see, and those men from the Hammer 'n' Tongs'll know booger-all on that score. This passage we're in is D3 minus two, or second spur on the right from the start of D3, but D3 minus four, which starts about forty yards further on, crosses underneath it, and minus two fell in on minus four where they cross paths, so now there's a hole between them."

"Are you sure?" said Garrett.

"Course I'm sure, ya silly booger," insisted Perkins. "I blasted out the minus four myself, didn't I. Bemis, you and Clemens go back out to the main line, find D3 minus four—you can use your helmet lamps —then go up the minus four spur 'til you get to the connecting passage, then go on through with your lamps off. Take the shovel, just in case the hole's stove in."

"Then what do we do?" I asked.

"When you're ready, switch on your lamps and come charging up-tunnel like your arses are on fire, talkin' on the radio like there's a dozen of you. We'll let them know we're still here, and once they see that they're trapped between us, they'll have no choice but to give themselves up."

"Or else go down with guns blazing," I said.

"Have you got a better idea, Clemens?" Perkins said.

I wasted no one's time claiming that I did.

Calvin and I and the shovel went out to the main line, turned on our headlamps, and worked our way down-tunnel to D3-4 (which was faintly but definitely marked as such), then started into it.

"We forgot to ask how far along it is," I said, by which I meant the connecting passage.

"We'll find it," was Calvin's terse reply. He would find it, anyway, because he was in the lead.

The spur was more snug than most, and soon we were walking bent almost double with the air cylinders on our backs scraping against the ceiling. We traversed one dogleg, then another, then after rounding a third, we came up against a pile of rubble.

"We're stuck now," I said.

But Bemis thought otherwise. "I think this is it, only the sides of the hole have fallen in. Hand me the shovel. "

I did so, and he used it to push the debris forward, then he stood up straight and I knew his head must be in the tunnel above us.

"Do you see them?" I said.

"No," he replied. "I'm switching off my lamp. You'd better do the same."

"Very well. Do we by any chance know which way is which?"

This, for once, stopped Calvin cold. After a while he gave in and said, "No. We'll have to guess."

He climbed into the tunnel above, which was a merciful few inches taller, and soon after I did the same.

"Can you see anything?" I said.

"Of course not," he said, a bit peevishly. Then, "Wait a minute while our night vision returns." All the night vision in the world will do you no good if there is no light at all, but I decided that Calvin didn't need to be reminded of that right then.

"There," he said suddenly. "We go this way."

"Which way is that?"

He said nothing, just pulled me in the direction he'd decided to go.

"Should we start the hullabaloo?" I asked, as we worked our way along the passage.

"Let's try to see if we're going the right way first," he replied, although I'd thought that question decided.

Then about a minute later Bemis went into a sharp dogleg. I knew this because I didn't, and ran up against the tunnel wall instead. "Calvin," I said, "if you could alert me to impending doglegs I would be —"

He let out a cry of alarm.

"Well, it's too late now," I said.

"Hell and damnation," he growled. These were mighty oaths for the likes of Calvin Bemis.

"Are they there?" I said. "Should we start the charge?"

"No, it's—just watch your step coming around."

I was about to ask how I was supposed to see my steps without any light when suddenly I saw them, my boots that is. He had turned on his headlamp and, as advertised, an effluvial fan of light spilled into the bend. I continued to keep my eyes firmly on my boots, as I'd been advised to do, and thus I nearly failed to fall onto the ground when my boot landed on an air cylinder.

"What the—"

"Shh."

Bemis was shushing me again. Had he found another ghost, I wondered.

No, what he had found, literally stumbled upon in fact, was a cache of supplies. In the light from his headlamp I counted eight air cylinders, plus a fat bag full of spare batteries, some delicious vacuum-frozen comestibles, a ten-gallon carboy of water, and what appeared to be a vacuum tent rolled up into a cylinder.

"Looks like our friends are planning to stay awhile," I whispered. "They've got—"

"Radios off," ordered Calvin.

He had turned his headlamp off as well, plunging us once again into complete blackness.

Our helmets somehow found each other in the dark, and Calvin's hollow booming voice said, "Sam, tell me if I'm wrong, but this changes everything."

"How's that?" I said.

"If we take their supplies and put them where they can't find them, we can starve them out," he explained.

"Or suffocate them out," I said.

"Exactly."

I liked this plan, because it held out the promise, or at least the possibility, of less sudden violent death than charging the enemy head-on—or even from the rear, as we were planning to do.

I said, "That's a splendid idea, Cal, but what about Perkins and Garrett? They're waiting for us to drive the devils into their trap."

"True," he said. "Perhaps if we go far enough along the tunnel in their direction, we can—wait," Calvin interrupted himself, "is that a lamp? Someone's coming this way! Back around the bend, Sam. Quickly."

He pulled my arm and we retreated around the dogleg.

He again held his helmet against mine and said, "They must be here to replenish supplies. They have no way of knowing we're here, and with lamps off and our radios switched back on, we'll be able to hear what they're saying without detection. If we can keep quiet, that is." I knew full well that the "we" he was referring to was me.

"Certainly," I agreed.

So I crouched in the tunnel, watching the play of light and shadow across the wall of the bend as if I were a denizen of Plato's celebrated cave, breathing as shallowly and quietly as possible, and listening for —listening for all I was worth. What I heard, like much of what I learned in the Moon, was interesting, generally unpleasant, and potentially rewarding if a great deal of effort was applied in putting it to use.

There were two men on the other side of the dogleg, which was convenient for conversation, as a man on his own was not likely to tell us much—

unless he happened to be John Jones, who was quite capable of holding up both ends of a conversation by himself. But there were two men, and what was better, they were arguing, although it was not clear at first what they were arguing about.

"We'll never hear the end of it from Black Johnny if we don't secure this spur," said one of the men. "T' say nothing of the whole line."

"Black Johnny can go straight to the devil," said the second. "And they ain't going nowhere in any case." I didn't understand who 'they' were, as yet, but I had no doubts whatsoever about who 'Black Johnny' was. Of course, if the men of the Hammer 'n' Tongs had been as handy with a moniker as they were at breaking and entering, their resident lunatic would surely have been called Black Jack, but I was in no position to correct them.

"I'll hold yer coat for ya while ya tells ol' Johnny where he oughta go, shall I?" said the first man. The second man made a rude but otherwise unintelligible noise over this, while the first continued speaking. "Black Johnny'll not be a factor. And I tell ya, those Deirdres'll be right there where we left 'em, hidin' out just around that bend. Now where'd ya put them bullets?" Apparently we weren't the only ones low on ammunition.

"They're in with the batteries," said the other. "If I was them I'd send a man around the 'leg firin' that pistol for all I was worth. If he was smart enough to keep his lamp out, we'd never know he was there 'til we was full a holes."

"So why d' ya think they ain't done it already, old cock? Cuz they ain't got the bullets is why." The man had guessed at our, or really Perkins's, dilemma, and he had guessed correctly. "You sure they're in here?" It took a moment for me to figure out he was talking about the bullets, not Garrett and Perkins. "Damn if there ain't—ah, here they are. Now hand over that pistol. Two c'n play at guns a-blazin', only if they had more bullets I 'spect we'd a heard plenty outta them by now."

Somehow we had to warn Perkins that these men were freshly loaded for Deirdres and ready to go on the attack, and in my agitation I had almost said as much to Bemis and "blown the gaff," as they say backstage at the carnival.

"Good thing Black Johnny gave over a pistol," said one, the one who had not consigned Black Johnny to the devil, I believe. And this was good news, of a sort. It appeared that they had only the one pistol after all.

"He ain't gonna need it where he's goin'," said the other, the one who had consigned Black Johnny to the devil. I must say that carrying a loaded pistol with you on your way into Hell is a notion pregnant with theological possibilities, but it is just as surely a question best left for another day. "Not with the dynamite he's carrying," said the same voice. Taking a box full of dynamite with you into Hades would up the ante considerably, and is worthy of further discussion. However, I soon began to suspect that Perdition was not Black Johnny's immediate destination, although it was hard to imagine that the proprietor of that notorious establishment didn't have his lodgings already set aside.

"Crazy as a shit-house rat, you ask me," said the other man.

"True enough," the first chuckled. "He'll put a quick end to these thieving Deirdres though, blowin' their resonance engine to kingdom come."

"Not the engine!" shouted Bemis.

Against all odds and expectations, it was Calvin who had blown the gaff.

"Who's that?" said the first man.

"Twern't me, Bob," insisted the second.

"Deirdres!" they shouted together.

Bemis, who knew full well that he was responsible, wasted no time in pushing me back down the tunnel. I wasted no time at all in complying. I went through the first dogleg at a run, or as close to it as I could manage in a pressure suit, with Calvin bumping me along from behind. I saw the walls around me light up suddenly then disappear again, and I knew they were firing the pistol at us. I plunged with even greater speed into the second, or perhaps it was the third, dogleg with Bemis still close behind me, then saw the reflection of another flash on the wall of the bend.

"Calvin, are you—"

"I'm all right," he interrupted. "Although I think a bullet hit one of my air cylinders. Just keep moving." I kept moving, running in total darkness, except for the occasional flash from the pistol.

This went along fine until I stepped into the hole, otherwise known as the improvised entrance into D3-4. I fell awkwardly into said hole, and Calvin, coming along right behind me, tripped over whatever parts of my haggis hadn't gone in yet, and fell on top of me.

"In, in!" he shouted, and I hurried to get the remainder of my haggis into the minuscule passage. Once I had moved a short distance up the minus four tunnel, Bemis leapt in, then stopped to pile up as much debris as possible into the space between himself and the hole, no doubt hoping this would discommode our pursuers.

After that we half-ran and half-crawled through the low tunnel, acting like a pair of gophers pursued by a cottonmouth. When we reached D3 itself, where we could nearly stand, we redoubled our pace, and in a remarkably short time we shot through the entrance to the D line, where several men stood doing nothing useful that I could see, except for one, who dealt me a ringing blow to the helmet with a shovel. The quick-witted imbecile wielding the shovel turned out to be Chalk.

"Chalk!" I hollered. "It's me. Clemens. Are you trying to kill me all over again?"

"My apologies, Samuel," he said. "Thought you was one a them."

"Well, that's something, I suppose," I said. "They're right behind us," I added more usefully. "And they're firing at us with a pistol, so be prepared. Where's the captain?"

"Was here, but he's gone off again," Chalk said.

"I'm going to warn Mister Lovelace," Calvin said, and departed immediately.

I looked around to take the measure of our forces. "Is Perkins still in the D3?" I asked. "And Garrett?"

"Far as we know," said Watkins, but he was wrong.

A moment later, a haggis came plunging through the sally port at a run, yelling, "It's me. Garrett. Perkins is right behind me." I could have tried this, and perhaps avoided a blow to the head, but I was busy and it hadn't occurred to me at the time.

Foolishly, I turned and looked down the tunnel, hoping to see Perkins trotting into the glare of our cluster of helmet lamps. Instead I saw a flash, then another, soon followed by the sound of a voice I knew well.

"Booger! Booger me. Booger booger booger!" Perkins dove across the threshold of the sally port just as another flash shone behind him—and a bullet, its energy fortunately largely spent, ricocheted off

Watkins's helmet. Perkins stood up, then threw the six-gun in his glove to the ground. "Out of boogerin' bullets."

"Unfortunately, they have plenty," I said.

"Oh, Clemens," he said. "Good to see you're all right. Where's Bemis?"

"He went to warn Mister Lovelace. You see, we found out that—"

"Captain!" Perkins cried, derailing my revelations. Merriwether stepped into the penumbra of lamplight in the antechamber. "Captain, do you have the other pistol? Or more ammunition at least?"

Captain Merriwether handed him the second six-gun without hesitation. Perkins immediately faced the sally port and peered into it, hoping, I'm sure, to spy something to shoot at.

Then Merriwether drew open a small sack and took out a stick of dynamite. "Can one of you men prepare this?" he said quietly. "My hands are trembling too much to secure the cap, I fear."

Much to my surprise, I reached over and took the sack and the dynamite from his gloves, saying, "I can do it, Captain. Mister Perkins has taught me how," and I opened the sack and began to assemble the charge.

"Thank you," he mumbled distractedly, then said, "Who is that?"

"Clemens, sir," I said.

He said, "Pleased to see you're learning, Clemens." Despite the pleasantries, I felt rather distinctly that I was attending a funeral, or at best a wake.

"What's that for, Cap'n?" said Chalk.

"To seal the D line," he said. Several of the men exclaimed in surprise.

"Never you fret now, Cap'n," said Chalk. "We'll stop 'em, sure's yer born. Ain't that right, Samuel?" I said nothing, being much preoccupied with preparing the D's destruction. "Why, we'll run 'em clear back ta Lucky Strike. You jus' give the word." This was big talk from a man who had spent the afternoon watching the sally port from the outside, but still I said nothing.

Captain Merriwether said, "Thank'y, Chalk, but that won't be necessary. This," he pointed at the dynamite I was preparing, "will keep them bottled up in the Ds while we pack our kit."

"Pack our kit?" said Winters, at least I think it was Winters. "Are ya sayin', sir, that we're to abandon ship? We can lick the bastards, Cap'n, honest we can." This from the other man who had spent the day outside the sally port.

"I have no doubt we could—you're a fine crew," said the captain. "But if they want the Deirdre so badly, then they can have it." This brought on a shower of protests from, as far as I could tell, everyone except me—my attention was largely confined to the dynamite—and Perkins, who was lurking somewhere beyond the mouth of the tunnel, still looking for something to shoot. No one wanted to come right out and call the captain a coward, not to his faceplate, but the accusation was as palpable as if the word had been carved into the wall.

"They want it all right, the nasty boogers." This was Perkins of course, still inside the D line, but clearly within radioing distance. "Do we have any more bullets?"

"Garrett. Watkins. One of you go help Mister Perkins to hold them off. And take some ammunition." A pair of helmets turned to face each other, and then one of them took up the pistol Perkins had discarded and the lone box of six-gun shells, and ran into the tunnel after him. Merriwether then turned to me. "Clemens, are you ready with that stick?"

"Yes, Captain," I said solemnly. "But I have no experience with laying a charge."

"That's fine," he said. "I'll place it." He took the stick of dynamite, with its blasting cap and attendant wiring attached, and I took up the spool, preparing to unreel the wire behind him. He took a step toward the entrance and the rain of objections began again.

The captain barked, "Stow it," then, once the protests had been duly stowed, he sighed and said, "Can't you men see, the Deirdre is played out." This precipitated yet another downpour of protests. "I didn't want to believe it either," he continued, once the squall had passed. "That's why I brought all this on us by reopening the D2—but it isn't any use, men. There's no ice left to be had in this hole. The Hammer 'n' Tongs boys can have it. They'll find nothing but rock."

There was still a light drizzle of objections, then Perkins's voice came over the radio. "Captain's right, boys, sorry to say. Right as rain." Not a drop of protest followed. "You know I'd tell you, I didn't think it were so, but the cap'n's steerin' you true. For better or worse, we're done here. Now let's have that dynamite in here before I get killed."

Captain Merriwether and the dynamite went through the sally port. A minute later, he, Perkins, and Garrett came back out, and the dynamite did not.

"Is everyone accounted for?" asked the captain.

"I believe so," Perkins said, "except—Clemens, where's Bemis?"

"Oh Lord," I said.

"Is he still in the D3?"

"No," I said quickly. "He went to help Mister Lovelace." By now, Merriwether had uncoiled a substantial length of wire and ordered everyone around the nearest dogleg. Taking my usual place face down on the ground, I continued, "While we were lurking in the D3 minus four—no, make that the minus two—we heard two of the devils say Black Johnny—that's their name for Jones—that Black

Johnny had gone to blow up the Deirdre's resonance engine."

"Sweet Jesus," said Merriwether. "But he can't do that."

"That's what they said," I insisted.

"Oh, the crazy bastard would try it no doubt, only there's no way he could have escaped the Ds. There's just the one way out and—" He paused significantly. "Chalk. Winters. Did you leave your post?"

"Why, never in life, Cap'n," said Chalk. "Hardly at all, Cap'n. Only once or twice ta have a piss and replenish our air."

"Deserting your post is a hanging offense, Gottschalk," growled the captain.

"'Twere only for a minute."

"I'm going to see if I can help Bemis," I said. I was fond of the resonance engine, to be sure, but Bemis— well, Bemis was my partner.

"Well, go help him then," Merriwether grumbled. "We'll all be along soon enough." I sensed from his tone that he was preoccupied—likely with selecting the cordage for Chalk's hanging. Of course hanging was too good for Chalk, at least in this case, because, despite all the good intentions in the world, hanging a man is a tedious and unfulfilling operation on the Moon, and the man on the business end of the rope is far more likely to laugh at your efforts than die as he should—inadequate gravitation being the culprit once again. No, on the Moon a nice firing squad is the thing. I hoped the captain was busy in his mind selecting the bullets.

I climbed to my feet and charged down the tunnel toward the airlock. Over the radio I heard the captain shout, "Fire in the hole," and even halfway back to the belowdecks I could feel the ground jump and tremble beneath my boots.

Chapter Ten

I reached the airlock and worked my way through in a minute or two, although it seemed to take the better part of an hour. I watched the needle on the 'lock's big pressure gauge crawl up to near fifteen pounds per square inch, then removed my helmet and cranked open the inner hatch. The electric bulb in the small chamber just inside was still alight, and from this I surmised that Jones hadn't destroyed the resonance engine, as yet. I plunged into the tunnel that led first to Mister Kent's galley and from there to the belowdecks. It was not strictly the fastest way to Mister Lovelace's realm, but I had realized that I had brought nothing with which to defend myself, let alone help Bemis and Lovelace to defend, or retake, the precious resonance engine, and I thought Mister Kent might provide something: perhaps a butcher's knife to wave around, or a pot of boiling slush to pour down the access shaft onto Black Johnny's head.

I found Mister Kent in an agitated state when I arrived, tugging furiously at his beard and "flitting from pillar to post," as my old nanny used to say.

"Clemens," he barked upon seeing me. Then, "Where's the captain? Where are the others?" I've never thought of myself as particularly vain or self-aggrandizing, yet I found that being greeted in this manner rankled a bit.

"They are busy blowing up the D line," I said. "Have you seen Calvin Bemis?"

"I have not," said Kent. "But I have met the notorious John Jones, I regret to say, and feel fortunate to have survived the encounter."

"Where is he?" I said anxiously, glancing around the cavern as if I might have overlooked him.

"I'm afraid I don't know," he said. "Fortunately, I'd set Mister Lang up in the hammock in the chicken coop—you know it well from your convalescence, I'm sure—and thus I was able to convince the villain that he had expired." Kent twisted his beard. "Otherwise I fear Jones would have shot him again."

"Clemens!" came a croaking cry from the direction of the chicken coop. I turned and walked the dozen or so steps to the tiny noisome chamber full of cackling hens. Despite all reasonable expectations, this closet had its own electric light, since it had been discovered that a hen will not lay if dawn never arrives, even if the daylight is only an electric bulb. Lang lay in the hammock, wrapped in a tattered blanket. "Clemens," he said, "where is the captain?" I resolved then and there to spend some time, when I could spare it, improving my efforts at self-promotion.

"Blowing up the D line," I said.

"Did you bring the pistols? I very much need to put a bullet into Jones before he destroys the

Deirdre." And with that he tried to climb out of the hammock.

Kent had followed me into the chicken coop, and he stepped to the hammock and gently but firmly held Lang in place. "No you don't, Percy," he insisted. "Not today. There's plenty of men can deal with Jones."

I felt profoundly foolish. A pot brimming with boiling oil would have provided drama and novelty, but securing one of Captain Merriwether's six-guns would have been the more prudent, and obvious, course. "I'm afraid not," I said.

Lang snapped, "My God. Then what the hell good are you, sir?" That was a question worth considering, I reckoned, but only after I'd found Calvin Bemis and saved the resonance engine.

I turned to Kent and said, "I gather from what you said earlier that Jones carried a pistol."

"Yes," said Kent. "And I believe he would have shot me, just for good measure, if he'd dared. He hates all Deirdres indiscriminately, I believe. I can only assume he didn't due to a shortage of ammunition."

I said, "What do we have that can be used as a weapon?"

"A knife perhaps?" he said, and he led me to his store of implements.

I selected the longest and most evil-looking of the items on offer, and made my way to the belowdecks, which was entirely free of loafing Deirdres for perhaps the first time in my experience. I saw Calvin's hastily discarded pressure suit lying on the deck, and following his lead I stripped mine off in record time. I would wish I'd left it on if Black Johnny succeeded in his awful mission, but the suit's extreme awkwardness when not pressurized (exceeded only by when it was pressurized, of course) argued against retaining it. I had managed to leave the helmet behind in the galley in any case, and without that, the remainder of my suit was useless. So, free of my haggis and with carving knife in hand, I ran to the steamy vestibule containing the shaft leading down to Mister Lovelace's engine room.

From the top of the shaft, all appeared copacetic to my untrained eye. I heard the usual cacophony of mechanical noises, and felt the expected miasma of wet steam rising from the shaft's mouth. Poised to brave the descent, I realized that, stripped as I was to my under-drawers, I had no place in which to sheath my weapon. So, feeling every inch the buccaneer, I clasped the knife between my teeth.

I then began to climb down the shaft, holding onto the center pole and proceeding hand-over-hand. However, after descending halfway to the opening above the engine room catwalk, I stopped, deciding that dropping into the chamber feet-first—stockinged feet first, in my fancy red under-drawers—was likely to make me conspicuous. I turned myself over and went the rest of the way upside-down—that is to say, head first. This maneuver would have been impossible for anyone but a trapeze artist on Earth, but in the Moon it is not only possible but reasonably easy to do.

After turning turtle, I crept down the shaft until my head was mere inches above the opening, and hung there like a bat. A singular bat to be sure: one sporting unruly red hair, a fine red mustache, bright red under-drawers, and a knife between its teeth. Steam-shrouded light filled the circle below me, and over the rumble and clatter of the still-churning machinery, I heard the unmistakable voice of Black Johnny Jones.

"Now, I don't want ta shoot you men, as you had no part in my demise, least as I remember. Still, I will if ya try ta stop me." This was in line with what Mister Kent had surmised. Black Johnny must have been cruelly short on bullets. After all, he had shot at me repeatedly without even knowing my name. In any case, it seemed clear that he indeed had a pistol, and it was almost certainly trained on Mister Lovelace, and likely Calvin Bemis as well.

I inched myself lower, until I could just see around the lower edge of the shaft, and there, still in his blackened haggis but without the helmet, stood Black Johnny. And providence was with me, because he was standing with his back to me when my head appeared. If he'd been facing my way, I fear that, despite the shortage of bullets, there would have been a new and darker shade of red added to my ensemble. As I'd expected, Calvin and Mister Lovelace stood beyond Jones, Bemis in under-drawers matching my own, and Lovelace in his usual overalls. I saw Calvin's eyes go wide upon seeing my bat imitation, but he caught himself immediately and feigned nonchalance thereafter. I could not tell from Mister Lovelace's expression whether he had seen me or not, which was just as well.

I have mentioned before that a typical pressure suit has no pockets. Jones's blackened haggis was no exception, and he had a canvas sack slung over one shoulder. I could tell from its contours that it held at least two sticks of dynamite.

Meanwhile, Black Johnny was holding forth like an after-dinner speaker deep in his cups, and Bemis and Lovelace seemed to be encouraging him in it— reckoning, I can only suppose, that Black Johnny talking them to death was a great deal better than Black Johnny blowing them to pieces.

"But, Jones," said Lovelace, "why aren't you dead?"

"Because I got the drop on ya, didn't I," said Jones.

"No, sir," corrected Lovelace. "I mean to say, how is it that you survived the collapse of, what is it, of D2?"

"Ya mean, what did I do once the tyrant Merriwether sent the roof down on me and left me for dead? Same as any man in my position woulda done. I screamed bloody murder at them, pleaded with them, cursed them, begged them for mercy, then damned them all to hell, but they'd wanted me dead all along and now they'd done it, so they—"

"It's not my department, but I believe the men dug out the tunnel after it collapsed," Lovelace said. "And your body—that is to say, you weren't there."

"I knew then it was a trap they'd laid for me—" Jones was saying.

"A trap?" said Bemis, urging him on.

"The cave-in, man. Don't tell me that was an accident. They meant to deal with their jonah, an' they did, the barstards. Did it in fine style. Only I weren't killed in the rock fall, was I, only my lamp busted and left in a dead-end spur with no way out. If'n that ain't dead, then I'd like ta know what is. I was mightily upset by then, ya could say, and damning the Deirdre and all who worked her to hell like they deserved, when I set a boot too far afield in the blackness and fell down into a hole." That accounted for the slush I'd seen on the crevasse's walls. "I lost my wits entirely then and don't recollect how I got there, but when I came to my senses I found myself at the bottom of that hole, least as far as I could tell with no lamp, and natur'ly I set to grieving over my fate at the hands of the accursed Deirdres, sending oaths abroad in the aether until I lost consciousness from lack of air, certain that Lang and Merriwether and the rest had kilt me dead at last."

As Jones told his story, I saw Bemis and Lovelace exchange a glance, and Calvin took a step sideways.

"Don't move, you," Jones growled, "else you'll taste a bullet."

Calvin stopped moving, but Jones took a step back, toward me. Gripping the pole with my legs, I took the knife from my teeth and held it poised, prepared to bushwhack Black Johnny should he come any closer. All that was lacking, as usual, was any knowledge of how to go about it.

"So why aren't you dead?" asked Lovelace a second time.

Black Johnny attempted a laugh and failed, to startling effect. "Hoist upon yer own bloody petard, aren't ya, ya thievin' barstards." I saw Bemis and Lovelace exchange another look, this time of puzzlement. "That's the Hammer 'n' Tongs territory down there. They heard my laments and cursing of the Deirdres and they come and dragged me out. Or so they told me later, seein' as I was largely insensible at the time."

As Jones spoke, Bemis continued to drift gradually to port. The excruciating level of nonchalance in his movements signaled, if only to me who knew his ways, that he was up to something.

"And I gather you've been planning your revenge ever since," Lovelace said. He scrupulously avoided looking at Calvin, so I knew he was in on it too, whatever it was.

Black Johnny said, "It's all that's kep' me goin' since ya kilt me, i'n't it. And now I'll be blowing up your precious engine here, to guarantee the Deirdre's end." He used the hand not holding the pistol to draw a bundle of three sticks of dynamite, with blasting cap already attached, from his sack. "And the two a you as well, seein' as you love the thing so. Then it's on to plant a bullet in Merriwether's gut, and that tattooed little troll Gottschalk after that." Then he glanced at the pistol in his glove. It was an exceedingly brief glance, but it exhibited what the gamblers call a "tell." I was suddenly certain he had only one bullet in the pistol, and he was saving it for Captain Merriwether if he could. What he said next only cemented my certainty. "I believe I'll throw the little barstard into the vacuum in his under-drawers an' watch his eyes pop outta his ugly head. But first it's the engine and the pair a you." Although I couldn't see anything of his face, it was clear from Black Johnny's tone that he was, after all those days and months of misery, at last enjoying himself.

"There's no call for that, Jones," Lovelace said. "You said yourself you didn't want to shoot us. And Mister Bemis here had no part whatever in your— troubles. He was not even in the Deirdre until several months ago."

"Ain't that too bad." Jones shook his head. "I said I didn't wanna shoot ya. I never said I didn't want you dead. No, I mean to kill the lot of ya, one way or the other."

"And how do you expect to get away then?" Lovelace asked, figuring, correctly as it happened, that Black Johnny would not be shy in detailing his plans for escape.

"How d'ya think? Once I've set the charge I'll jump up the shaft and set 'er off from yer accursed belowdeck. I got plenty a wire, haven't I." And as he said this he pulled a spool from the sack. "Enough talk," he barked. "You, the new man." He aimed the pistol at Bemis. "You keep well back now, and stay the professor here, or else he'll have a bullet." As he spoke, he waved the hand holding the dynamite, and I watched the blasting cap pitch about as he did so. I silently exhorted it to work itself loose, but alas it did not.

Meanwhile, Calvin had moved several feet to one side, while Lovelace held his position in front of Jones. He was no nearer to Jones and the dynamite than he'd been before, but considerably closer to a collection of hoses and valves leading from the boiler, each valve with its attendant gauge standing guard above it. Calvin glanced at a gauge, then directly at me. Jones saw the direction of his glance and started to turn to see who or what might be behind him, when Calvin reached out, gripped a thick hose in both hands, and yanked it free from its housing. He yowled in pain—apparently the hose was rather hot —then ducked and fell to the catwalk as a geyser of steam hissed from the exposed valve. The fountain of scalding-hot steam caught Black Johnny just on the neck ring of his haggis and spattered gobs of soot-blackened slush into the air. He screamed and staggered backward, and I knew that at last my time had come.

I turned over, released the pole, fell down into the engine room, and landed on Black Johnny's back, holding onto the pair of air cylinders he had not taken the time to remove. He roared his shock and defiance, and simultaneously fired the pistol. I thought I heard the tinkle of shattering glass over the clatter of machinery and hiss of boiling steam, then I saw a new, nearly invisible geyser of foul-smelling gas spray into the cavern. I tried to bring my long-cherished carving knife to bear on Black Johnny's scalded neck, but he spun and shot up toward the roof of the cavern, with me still aboard. (Leaping involuntarily into the air, and finding yourself out of reach of anything with which you might improve your trajectory, is all too common on the Moon.) I tried once again to bring the knife to its business, but my wrist struck a pipe, and the knife flew out of my hand and was soon lost amongst the confusion of machinery below.

The smell in the engine room was suddenly that of Hades, and Lovelace shouted, "He's punctured the waste reclamation tank. The hydrogen sulfide you smell is highly flammable, Jones. Fire again and you'll kill us all." This, in my judgment, might have served more as an inducement for Black Johnny than a cause for restraint, but then in my judgment he was also out of bullets. Still, breathing the gas that was flooding the chamber might produce the same result, only slower.

As if to verify my prediction, I saw Mister Lovelace collapse to the catwalk, and in the same moment, as Jones hollered and twisted and flailed his encumbering haggis to shake me loose, Calvin shouted, "Can you hold him, Sam? I have to get Mister Lovelace up the shaft."

I had no idea how long I could entertain Black Johnny. Until he managed to kill me, I supposed. He caught hold of a vertical pipe as we fell back toward the catwalk, and used the leverage to whirl around and slam my unprotected body against the upper side of the resonance engine. I felt the prominent knobs, gauges, and presumably the very verniers themselves dig into my back.

"I—I'll try," I said, but what I really wanted was to determine the current location of the dynamite. Had he dropped it when I'd attacked him? Then I saw that the sticks, with the blasting cap in place, were still in his left hand, clutched to the chest of his pressure suit and dripping with black slush. It was fortunate that I was holding tight to his air cylinders, the only part of him not slippery with grease.

"Let go a me, ya barstard!" Jones hollered, and slammed me against the gauges again. He held the vertical pipe with one hand and the dynamite with the other—so I had been correct, I thought—he had tossed away the pistol in favor of a handhold, so clearly all its bullets had been spent.

Six or so feet below us, I saw Calvin carry Lovelace (conscious or not, I could not tell) to the escape shaft, place the engineer's arms around the pole, and throw him bodily up the shaft.

Then he looked over his shoulder, more or less in my direction, and shouted, "You can let him loose now, Sam." He looked above him into the dark vertical hole, and appeared satisfied by what he saw. At least Lovelace hadn't fallen back and landed on him, so something was going right. Still, I was far from certain that letting loose of Black Johnny was a good idea. The steam inside the engine room was very thick by then, but apparently Bemis could see me being beaten against the side of the resonance engine like a carpet at spring cleaning, and concluded that I might be in need of some help. And suddenly he was holding Black Johnny's pistol. I assume he pulled the trigger and got no satisfaction, although I felt a sliver of it over being right.

He shouted, "Duck, Sam!" and threw the pistol at Black Johnny's head. As I had obediently ducked, and closed my eyes for good measure, I didn't see where or how the pistol landed, but I heard Jones yelp with pain, then bellow with rage, and knew Calvin had hit the mark.

Jones released his grip on the pipe and fell to the catwalk. I let go of him in mid-flight and landed awkwardly on one foot in front of him, teetering on my toes like a prima ballerina, then leapt at the opening to the shaft, into which Bemis had just disappeared. I grabbed the center pole as I shot past— even experienced men invariably overshoot any leap made on the Moon—and thus spun myself around it, only to see Black Johnny, now on his feet, prepare to leap after me. I glanced up into the dark hole above me, saw that Bemis had successfully vacated the premises, bent my legs, and shot upward, raising my hands to guard against hitting my head on the ceiling at the top of the shaft, since of course I had pushed off with too much force. Then, just as I saw light at the upper end of the tunnel, an arm reached down and grabbed me by the hair, my luxuriant red hair, and pulled. This was help I did not need, or so I thought for the better part of a second, then another hand grabbed my ankle from below, on the leg that had recently been abused of course. So Black Johnny had me by one end and, presumably, Calvin Bemis had me by the other. I continued moving upward, however, and soon Bemis had pulled me out of the shaft entirely, and Jones, still clutching my ankle, came half out of it as well, smearing the edge of the shaft with wet black slush as he came. There was a crowd of men gathered about the top of the shaft, most still in their pressure suits, helmets held by one glove. Black Johnny let go of my ankle and staggered to his feet, or to his boots, as the case may be.

Someone more observant than I said, "He's still got the dynamite."

"That's right, ya barstard," Jones said, "so you'd best keep well back." He paused and appeared to consider a moment, then said, "Still, yer engine's gotta go, an' I got plenty a wire, don't I." He held the electrical condenser that would detonate the blasting cap in one hand and the sticks of dynamite in the other, and after a second he tossed the dynamite into the hole. As the deadly package fell, the wires uncoiled, and Jones, along with all the rest of us, saw that they had got themselves looped around one of his boots. Perkins raised his helmet in a bid to hit Jones over the head when he bent to pull the wires loose, but just as Perkins swung, Jones slipped on the slush at his feet. He pitched forward, dropping the slush-coated condenser, Perkins's helmet sailed over his head, and he fell down into the shaft after his dynamite, cursing as he went. The condenser fell to the deck and Bemis made a grab for it, but then it jerked, flew up, and struck the pole in the center of the shaft. I saw a spark, and an instant later there came a deafening clap of thunder, and a combination of smoke, flame, foul air, and perhaps parts of Black Johnny Jones erupted out of the hole.

All the men, including me, were flung entirely out of the vestibule by the blast, and found ourselves scattered around the belowdecks like autumn leaves, singed by the flame, coughing and choking on the noxious fumes, and our ears ringing from the force of the explosion. I looked around me and saw—nothing. The electric bulb thereabouts had been extinguished in the blast, along with the rest of the electrical systems, our source of heat, and most cruelly, our source of air.

Chapter Eleven

"Get your pressure gear on!" shouted Perkins.

Fortunately, most of the men still wore their pressure suits. They quickly donned helmets and started their air, and soon thereafter several headlamps came alight, casting beams that swung about in the smoke like lighthouse beacons trying to pierce a thick fog. I scrambled over to where I'd left my haggis and began to climb into it. Bemis was doing the same beside me, while Mister Lovelace ran to collect his little-used gear from the airlock chamber where it was stowed. While suiting up, I automatically reached for my helmet, then remembered I'd inadvertently left it with Mister Kent. The air was exceedingly foul in the belowdecks, even at that early stage of the Deirdre's demise, and I tried to hold my breath for as long as I could stand while I worked to get inside my suit. Then I leapt up and ran into the tunnel leading to the galley, coughing up smoke and dust as I went. The air grew gradually better as I approached Mister Kent's chambers, and I was able to enter the galley breathing in a more or less normal fashion, but I knew that luxury would not be available for much longer.

"Clemens," cried Mister Kent, "thank goodness you're here." Now that was a greeting I could grow accustomed to, I thought. "Mister Lang is going to need some assistance getting into his pressure suit, and you might help me as well, if you will. I must admit that I spend as little time inside of a pressure suit as is possible, considering my circumstances. I find them—uncomfortably confining." He had unearthed a haggis, presumably his own, from somewhere, and had activated its headlamp, otherwise I could have seen nothing. Using its light, I retrieved my own helmet, placed it over my head, sealed it, and started the flow of air. Its metallic tang tasted sweet after sampling the smoky residue of the exploded resonance engine. I wondered, in passing, how long my present supply of air would last, and where exactly the next life-preserving cylinder would come from.

Kent was twisting the strands of his great beard into locks, then using bits of twine to tie these together into festoons. He continued speaking as he performed these strange ablutions, and despite being sealed into my dear haggis, I found I could still hear him in muted tones, since there was still air, if only of a poor sort, beyond my faceplate.

He said, "I assume from the darkness and the increasingly unhealthful atmosphere that you have failed to save the resonance engine." I wanted to assure him that, although what he'd said was true, the failure had not been entirely mine. But, since the statement was likely rhetorical, and further, since I suspected that any reply originating from within my haggis would be unintelligible, I only nodded my helmet in his direction and went to assist Mister Lang.

He lay on the filth-strewn floor of the now un-illuminated chicken coop—not a place anyone would choose to lie down if he could help it—and fought to get his wounded limb into the leg of his suit, grunting and grimacing with the pain of the effort.

"Clemens." His voice came faintly through my sealed helmet. "Thank heavens." I wondered briefly if I should frequent more disasters. "Help get me into this, will you? Kent is worse than useless."

I crouched down and untangled the suit's legs, and repositioned the boots, which were already attached, so that the haggis would behave itself upon Lang's arrival. I saw that someone—presumably Lang himself, upon resuming consciousness—had patched the bullet hole in the thigh. Tend to your pressure gear first, and bind up your own wounds when you find the time; that is a motto to stay alive by in these parts. I slowly pulled Lang's suit up his legs and over his hips, then assisted him into the upper section as well, as he was still more or less lying down. He checked the seals, secured his helmet, and almost immediately began speaking again.

I switched on my radio. "—Jones had his revenge? Is Mister Lovelace—"

I interrupted, in order to move things along. "Black Johnny destroyed the entire engine room, I expect. He carried three sticks of dynamite."

"Good Lord." Lang made as if to rise, so I helped him to his feet. "Black Johnny?" he said.

"That's what the men of the Hammer 'n' Tongs called Jones."

"I see. How many were killed? Is Mister Lovelace still—"

"As far as I know, only Jones was killed," I said. "But the Deirdre itself is finished, I'm afraid."

"You should have let me put a bullet into him," he growled.

"It was not up to me," I said. "How to employ the pistols, that is."

"I see that," he said. "Only they're your pistols, you know. We were unarmed before you and Bemis arrived." So the captain's precious pistols were really our precious pistols, once upon a time. No wonder everyone in authority kept asking me if I could hit anything with them.

I left the coop then, wondering for an instant what would become of the chickens. I wished the scrofulous rooster, who had performed his tedious arias non-stop during my convalescence, a swift trip to the devil, but I feared for the hens, expecting that, short of an heroic rescue, they would end their excursion to the Moon as vacuum jerky, feathers and all.

I returned to the galley to find Mister Kent stripped to his red under-drawers. With his ample girth, voluminous beard, and those red drawers, he looked like Kris Kringle, albeit a bewildered Kris Kringle gone wildly off course in his yuletide rounds. I helped him get into his pressure suit, as requested, taking particular care that the festoons of beard were not snagged on the neck ring when the helmet locked into place.

Meanwhile, Mister Lang said, "We have to gather up everything of value, especially water, air cylinders, foodstuffs, spare parts, and tools, and get it to the belowdecks, or better yet, take it directly to the airlock. It's a shame we don't have the hods to haul it, but they were all in the D line. Wrap as much of it as you can in blankets, or anything you can find." True to his word, he began piling pots, cooking utensils, a sack of beans, and an assortment of unruly root vegetables onto his former bedclothes. He added, "Hammocks will serve best for transporting the larger items." Lang was what the gamblers loafing in the texas would have called a "cool customer"— obviously in considerable pain, but out of his sickbed and directing the evacuation pretty much without pausing for breath.

Mister Kent, on the other hand, was nearly hysterical.

Panic, if not promptly checked, is as good as a death sentence when inside a pressure suit, and I immediately went about settling him down—not by directing him to calm himself, since that is rarely effective, but by diverting his attention to something else, preferably something that wasn't about to try to kill him.

"What shall we do about the livestock, Mister Kent?" I said.

"Livestock? What livestock?" Make the panicked man think, if you possibly can. "W-we have no livestock, Clemens." He paused. "We had a goat once upon a time, but it liked to chew at the men's air hoses, so we were obliged to eat it."

"The chickens," I said. "Is there a way to save them, do you think? If nothing else, they are meat on the hoof. So to speak."

"True," said Kent, almost chuckling, which was an excellent sign. "But I'll be damned if I know how to do it. They're surprisingly robust—I believe they actually like it here—but I doubt they could survive for any length of time in the vacuum." Kent's voice faltered then. "Will there be a pressure tent available for the return trip to civilization, Percy? That would suit the hens admirably, and honestly, myself as well. I fear I'll go mad if I have to remain in this—thing—for even a fraction of the trip. And you—your wound will need attention as well."

Lang said, "I'll see what I can do, Mister Kent. Now you'd best collect up your medicines and the like."

"Very well," Kent said. "May I remove the helmet for a spell?"

"You may not," said Lang definitively, then added, "What we need is a spare pressure suit."

"What for?" I asked.

"For the livestock, Clemens."

"Oh. Yes," I agreed, soon grasping his intentions.

"The problem would be getting them inside it," Lang said.

"Chalk might be able to help with that," said Kent, who was busy loading a trunk, and seemed to have himself under control for the moment. "The birds seem to like him more than most."

"Due to a similar cast of mind, no doubt," said I.

"No doubt," agreed Kent.

Lang said, "He's a better miner than you are, Clemens, and perhaps the best I've ever seen at moving about on the surface."

I said, "He's a genius at Lunar terpsichore. I'll grant him that."

"What's a topsy-turvy then, Samuel?" came Chalk's distinctive voice, and a second later a small grease-streaked haggis hove into view at the mouth of the forward tunnel. He was also a prodigy at sneaking up on a fellow, I decided.

"Oh, Chalk," Lang said. "Start hauling all this kit to the airlock. I'll stay put for now and continue loading supplies into hammocks and the like. Mister

Kent assures me I'll pay dearly for it if I run around on this leg."

"Aye, Mister Lang," answered Chalk.

"Clemens, you go with him," Lang said, then added, "Chalk, is there a spare pressure suit in stores?"

"Well now," said Chalk, "I believe the cap'n keeps a extra set a gear. He's in the belowdecks now, directing the men how ta go about abandoning ship, an' I'll ask after it if ya likes. Who should I say is to be wearin' it?"

"We thought it might suit the chickens," I said.

"Dear me," said Chalk. "Not sure how that'll suit the cap'n."

"Never mind that. Just bring it here," said Lang. "Now start moving this kit."

Chalk and I each took up as much in the way of supplies as we could manage, the limiting factor being not the weight, which was negligible as usual, but the size of one's bindle compared to the tunnel's stingy diameter.

We negotiated the passage in question and dropped our loads in the antechamber before the airlock, which was already piled high with hastily wrapped goods from the belowdecks. All the scene needed for Christmas was a fresh-cut fir tree and Mister Kent prancing around it in his under-drawers. Chalk then went in search of the captain's spare haggis, while I started up the passage leading to the belowdecks. I didn't get far before I ran into Calvin Bemis coming the other way, dragging a hammock piled high with air cylinders—and piled rather too high, I decided, since a party of them would jump ship whenever the hammock hit a rough patch. I suppose by now I don't need to tell you how many of those there were.

I would have had to demolish the entire unruly edifice of cylinders, and somehow dispose of Bemis as well, in order to get by, so I bowed to the inevitable and backed out of the passage, meanwhile collecting any cylinders and other gear that had gone overboard and fetched up within my reach.

"I can only hope these are all full," I said of the air cylinders. It was the rigorously enforced custom of the Deirdres to refill any and all cylinders depleted during their forays into the tunnels immediately upon returning to the belowdecks. Bemis and I had failed to do this when in pursuit of Black Johnny, however, and I suspected others had made the same mistake.

"Most are, but there're a few that are low. Be sure to check the gauge before you try one on," he said. I checked a gauge and found that I was carrying one of the miscreants in my arms. "Sam," Calvin said, then he paused portentously.

"Yes, Calvin?" I prompted.

"Sam, Captain Merriwether is planning on taking all the Deirdres back to Lucky Strike. And once there, he intends to pay each man what he's owed and return to New England."

"That's more or less what I had expected," I said, then looked around to find that I'd backed myself all the way to the airlock chamber. I selected a vacant spot beside a pyramid of water containers and began to unship the air cylinders that had not deserted the hammock during the trip. While doing this I noticed that my headlamp was going dim, and soon found that I could worry over spent batteries just as easily as I could over depleted air cylinders.

"So what do you think about that?" Calvin pressed.

As for that conversation, I was thoroughly in the dark. I placed the final cylinder on top of its fellows, stood up straight, and said, "What are you driving at, Calvin?"

"Well, I don't know about you, Sam, but that's not where I want to go."

"So where is it you—" Light dawned like I'd just installed a fresh battery. "Ahh," I said, "Now that you mention it, neither do I. I could never forgive myself if I had to go back to picking."

"I still intend to go prospecting," he said affirmatively. "And now that we know something about how it's done, our prospects should improve."

"Calvin," I marveled, "was that a pun?"

"What? Sam, do you want to go prospecting or not?"

"Absolutely, Calvin. Positively, unequivocally, and without a doubt. Despite the fact that, thanks to the Deirdre, I now know better." Then I had a thought, and right away it began to worry at me, pushing the empty air cylinders and depleted batteries temporarily to the back of the line. I said, "Will Merriwether want the Beast, do you think?"

"He'd better not," Bemis said.

And Chalk reappeared, carrying a fine-looking pressure suit slung across his shoulders.

I said, "It's a matter of how well fixed we are for supplies, I should think." I waved an arm at the loot surrounding us.

"If they have a working resonance engine and water enough, they should be fine," Bemis said. "Then again, we'll need plenty of water for the Beast."

I said, "Chalk, do you know if the digger Garrett and Watkins arrived in is operational?"

"I reckon so," he said. "But I's hardly the one ta be askin' that of. I come ta tell ya, cap'n wants all hands to muster here at the airlock in half a glass, ready to leave."

"How long is that?" asked Bemis.

"Fifteen minutes, if the sand is falling on Earth," I said.

"I'm after the hens then," Chalk added. "I 'spect the cap'n'll not object too strenuous once he sees they's already stowed."

I helped Bemis collect the wayward cylinders, batteries, spare hoses and the like that had deserted his hammock, saying as I did so, "In any case, Calvin, Merriwether refused the Beast when he was given the opportunity, and I for one say he has missed his chance."

"True enough," Bemis said. "But if he can't be persuaded to part with enough water, we'll have no choice but to go with him."

"There's time enough to fetch one last load from the galley," I said. "We'll inform the others of our intentions at the muster."

The first thing I saw upon entering the galley—I had purloined a fresh battery out of the Christmas heap, thinking it my due for the labor of transporting it—was a hen soaring majestically over the cookstove, with the cacophonous rooster in hot pursuit, and Chalk not far behind, none of them within six feet of the deck. As I watched, several more hens joined in the fun.

Back home, the chicken, in all the varieties I am familiar with, is considered a flying creature only as a matter of courtesy, but once established in the Moon, your typical hen is suddenly the equal of an eagle or an albatross in the matter of flight, or believes she is anyway, and is often rather full of herself over the fact.

Chalk was handicapped in his pursuit of the hens by being encased in a bulbous pressure suit, but at least he had tolerable air to breathe. The birds were far more nimble in their aerial acrobatics (although Chalk was not half bad), but were clearly starting to feel the effects of the foul atmosphere, which I expect by then consisted mostly of useless nitrogen, the deadly carbons monoxide and dioxide, smoke and dust particles for body, and a smattering of exotic poisonous gases for flavor.

Mister Kent, fortunately still inside his suit, stood surrounded by the remaining supplies, waving his arms and offering encouragement, if no real assistance, to Chalk in his game with the hens.

"Chalk," I said, "you're simply entertaining them with those antics, you know."

"And how would you go about catching them then, Samuel?" he said, lunging at a hen.

"I wouldn't try," I insisted.

Chalk managed to grab one of the hens by her feet, but it was only a moment before she slipped through his sausage-link fingers and soared free, cackling wildly, whether out of spite or in triumph over her escape I am not expert enough to say.

"So you'll be leavin' them ta expire then, I suppose," said Chalk as he fell back to the ground. "And it bein' your wondrous idea ta begin with." Then he clucked his disapproval, sounding uncannily like a hen.

"I suggest you place yon haggis on the deck, then toss in a handful of their preferred grub."

"And what's a haggis then?"

I reached out and lifted the captain's spare pressure suit off the floor.

"I expect they're a mite sharp-set by now," I continued, "not to mention intoxicated by the noxious air. Once the cock crosses the neck ring in pursuit of his supper, the hens will follow."

My scheme was so obviously enlightened that he did not even comment upon it, but went straight away in search of chicken feed. A minute later, I had positioned the haggis, Chalk applied the bait, and the rooster, whom I had looked forward to dining upon, even as vacuum jerky, led his charges through the neck ring and into the trap.

Easing the last of the six hens inside—by then they were staggering about like drunken sailors, thanks to the bad air—Chalk secured the helmet, inflated the suit, and, accompanied by copious if muffled cackling, said, "A clever ruse, Samuel, if I do say so. You'd best not advertise yer skills so boldly, though, else you'll find yerself Jimmy Ducks by 'n' by, an' that's a fact."

"Who is Jimmy Ducks?" I said.

Chalk chuckled as he raised the bloated, squirming, crowing haggis onto its empty boots. "Like I says, you are, mate, 'less I miss my guess. Jimmy Ducks is what we calls the man minds the poultry aboard ship. Now, you an' Mister Kent take up the rest a the kit, if ya will, whilst I escort these beauties ta the airlock." He grasped the suit and slung it over his shoulder.

"It sounds like easy duty to me," I said, filling Mister Kent's outstretched arms with a large bundle full of cans and dried food. "But I expect these birds will be taking up residence in Lucky Strike before long. Eggs were going for two dollars apiece last time I was there."

"And what about you, then?" asked Chalk.

"Well, I'd hope to fetch at least a sawbuck for any egg I might lay," I said.

"You're not goin' back then? Is that what yer sayin'?"

"No," I said. "I mean yes, that's what I'm saying. I came up here for the prospecting, and that is what I aim to do, given half a chance." I picked up the remaining bundles, shoved the heavily-laden Mister Kent gently into the tunnel's mouth, and left the dark, emptied galley behind.

There was barely room enough to stand once the last of us got into the airlock's antechamber, so great was the wealth of swag piled there, and in fact several of the men had perched upon the heaps to leave room for the rest of us. Headlamps were off, ostensibly to save the batteries, and a single electric lantern illuminated the chamber from atop a mound of spare parts.

Chalk was the last to arrive, and he immediately captured Captain Merriwether's attention.

"Chalk," Merriwether called, radio crackling, "what are you doing with my extra suit?"

"Which it's housin' the poultry, Cap'n."

"The chickens, in my suit? Chalk, you chuckleheaded imbecile, what—"

"It were Samuel's idea, Cap'n."

"I don't care if—" Merriwether began.

"Actually, it was my idea, sir," said Mister Lang. "Waste not want not was my thinking." It was my thinking, technically speaking, but at that moment Lang was welcome to it.

Captain Merriwether's sigh was loud over the radio. "Very well, Mister Lang. You will be responsible for the suit's salvage, should we ever need to put a man inside it. Now, everyone is present, I see, so we shall—"

"Oh dear," said a voice, likely that of Watkins, "not everyone, Captain. What's to become of poor Puss. Have any of you seen—"

"Good God!" the captain exploded. "Mister Lang is shot and grievously wounded, the resonance engine is destroyed, the very Deirdre itself must be abandoned, and all you men concern yourselves with is the welfare of a brood of hens and the damnable ship's cat."

"Fear not, Cap'n," said Chalk then. "Puss is berthin' with me."

"I don't care if she's—What? Where?" said the captain. "Not in with the chickens, surely."

"No, sir," said Chalk. "Like I says, she's bunkin'
with me. Toe the line fer muster now, Puss." Chalk
put a glove to his chest and a moment later a tiny,
complacent, black and white feline face with two
shining green eyes stared out of Chalk's faceplate
alongside the whaler's unshaven chin.

"Booger all," said Perkins, "How—"

"I don't mind, Mister Perkins. She ain't no bother."

"I expect not," said Perkins. "It's how Puss can
stand it worries me." He was rewarded with laughter
all around, even from Chalk, I believe.

For my part I had never taken on a passenger
anywhere near as substantial and importunate as a
full-grown cat. In fact, the only passengers I had
entertained aboard my haggis were fleas. These were
un-ticketed customers of course, stowaways if you
will, yet I found that I did not object to their custom
overly much. And upon reflection, I will say that one
can do worse in the matter of passengers than a circus
of fleas. They invariably travel light, with nary a
steamer trunk among them, they consume very little
in the way of ship's stores, cheerfully drink whatever
is to hand, and are exceedingly versatile in their
choice of accommodations, rarely occupying any
particular berth for above two seconds at a stretch—
and unlike barflies, they make no noise to keep the
pilot awake.

The captain returned to business then, saying,
"Now we have two diggers outside, both with

working resonance engines, as well as the traction engine that powers the dust boat. The diggers can haul the kit, and the steam tractor can pull its usual platform with a tent on board."

"Thank God," said the tremulous voice of Mister Kent.

"The diggers belong to the men, Captain," said Mister Lang then.

"Yes, I'm aware of that," Merriwether said. Then, "How are you holding up, Percy?"

"I'll be fine, sir," he replied. "But the wound will need re-dressing before very long. I'm smelling fresh blood."

Then Bemis said, "Captain Merriwether, Sam and I don't wish to return to Lucky Strike. We came out to find our fortunes in ice, and—" Here Bemis ran out of steam, but the gauntlet was on the ground for all to see nonetheless.

"I see," said Merriwether. "It's not my place to deny you what is rightfully yours, and you have performed well and earned your way. Still—" he paused, then said, "Mister Lovelace, can the resonance engine in the digger belonging to Garrett and Watkins produce enough oxygen for—" He took a moment to count the sausages that encased his fingers. "For nine men?"

There was no immediate response to his enquiry. I looked to where Lovelace's spotless haggis slumped against the chamber's rough-hewn wall.

The captain said, "Mister Lovelace, are you unwell?" There was still no response. "Someone check to see if his radio's working."

"I am with you, Captain," said the engineer at last, in a tone reminiscent of Black Johnny's when sunk into a trough of despair. "It's only the work and sweat of half a lifetime that's gone."

"I am heartily sorry for it, Mister Lovelace," said the captain.

"Gone in an instant," the engineer mourned. "Years of careful, even pioneering engineering, reduced to scrap and ashes in a moment. And for what? For nothing. Simply the whim of a madman." He stopped speaking then, and a sound I had never before heard from inside a pressure suit came over the radio. Lovelace was weeping for his lost machine.

Merriwether said, "Let us leave Mister Lovelace to compose himself. Mister Perkins, what is your opinion? Can the one resonance engine support the needs of nine men for the, say, four days it will take us to reach Lucky Strike?"

Perkins was also slow to respond. Finally, he said, "I expect it might, sir, given enough water, but then that may not be strictly necessary." He paused, and for some reason no one else spoke to fill the silence. "It may only have to accommodate eight men," he said at last. "I'd like to go with Clemens and Bemis, if they'll have me."

"Mister Perkins—" the captain began.

"The Deirdre is lost, Captain. 'Twas played out even before John Jones and the men of the Hammer 'n' Tongs came calling. You've told us as much yourself. My commission with the Deirdre is up, as I see it, and still I've not struck it big in the Moon, as they say, not big enough for my liking anyway. But of course it's up to the two of them if they'll have me."

Perkins was probably the most knowledgeable, and certainly the most enterprising, of the Deirdres, as I weighed them, whether it be with a stick of dynamite or a six-gun. He would be worth two of Calvin Bemis, I suspected, and a round half-dozen of myself, particularly in the matter of prospecting and operating a mine.

"I for one would be honored to have Mister Perkins aboard," said I.

"Absolutely," agreed Calvin. "Most definitely welcome."

"Thank you, men," Perkins said. "I'll do my best for you."

"I'll sign on as well then, if I might." It was Chalk who'd said this, of all people.

"Chalk?" I said. "Why should you want to—"

"Ever since I saved yer life that time in the D line —ya remembers that, don'cha, Samuel?"

"Oh yes. Vividly," I assured him.

"Ever since that day, I's felt kinda responsible for ya, shipmate. I couldn't rest on me gold—what little there is of it, mind ya—back in Gloucester, with you an' Calvin still diggin' in the Moon. T'wouldn't be right, ya see."

"Oh, to the devil with you then," Merriwether barked. "Is there anyone else wants to desert me? If so, let's hear it now."

I said, "This means we take on Puss as well, I suppose."

"We'll need a tent then, since only two can fit into the cabin," said Bemis—and I knew the deed was done.

"Anyone else?" Merriwether repeated. "Don't forget that there's gold waiting for all of you men back on Earth. Even Bemis and Clemens have a share."

There was silence for a moment, then someone said, "What's that noise?"

I held my breath and listened. I heard a faint rhythmical squeaking which at first meant nothing to me, but after a few seconds Perkins identified it.

"Booger me," he whispered. "That's someone opening the airlock."

Chapter Twelve

For a moment I heard only the faint squeak of the airlock's outer hatch wheel turning and the sound of eleven men breathing softly in their suits. Then Perkins said, "Where're the pistols? Who has the pistols?"

"Who is it?" someone said.

"That'll be the men of the Hammer 'n' Tongs, no doubt come to rob us of what they can," said Captain Merriwether wearily. "Will we never stop paying for my heedless cupidity?"

Tossing supplies in all directions, Perkins barked, "I ask you again. Have any of you seen the boogerin' pistols?"

"My apologies, Mister Perkins," said Merriwether. "I've stowed them with my personal kit." He rummaged in a hammock-shrouded bundle and drew out the two weapons.

Next there came a distant rattling, and the slowly dying hiss of escaping air.

"They've opened the 'lock," said Mister Lang from where he lay supine upon the vacuum jerky.

The captain handed both of the pistols to Perkins. Perkins kept one for himself and passed the other to Bemis, who took it in his gloves, saying as he did so, "Will you pass over the ammunition please, Captain."

Merriwether did not reach for his kit. Instead he said, "There is none, Mister Bemis. We have only those shells that are left in the chambers."

"Can they hear us, do you suppose?" came a warning from someone more perspicacious than I.

Calvin cracked open his pistol, exposing its six chambers. All were empty. Perkins held up the second reputed weapon a moment later, and dashed our hopes by showing us that it was as innocent of bullets as the first. He muttered, "And there I was, blazing away like there was no tomorrow."

The faster squeak of the outer hatch being dogged shut could only be heard as vibrations coming through metal, since the air had been let out of the 'lock; still, I recognized the sound.

"The pistols are fully loaded," said Lang quite distinctly.

"Thank you, Mister Lang," intoned the captain.

A valve screeched open, and again there came the sound of moving air. This time it was a portion of our own deeply perverted atmosphere rushing in to fill the 'lock.

"They'll have a rude surprise if they expect to breathe for long in here," said Mister Kent.

The hissing of air subsided, and the wheel attached to the big sheet of aluminum that was the inner hatch began to turn. All eleven remaining Deirdres stood, lay, or crouched where they were, staring silently at the airlock.

"Should we block the hatch?" someone said at last.

"No," whispered the captain. "That would be fruitless. We need to get away more urgently than they need to get in."

Ten or so seconds later the hatch swung toward us, pushing some of our Christmas presents aside as it came. Four helmet lamps shone out of the airlock, their combined light thoroughly blinding us for a moment. They had plenty of charged batteries, then, I thought. Either that or they were fools. Or perhaps they thought to intimidate the Deirdres with such a spectacle. Was there another phalanx of miners waiting beyond the outer hatch, I wondered, or were these men the whole of the invasion force? After I got used to staring into those lamps, I saw that one of the men held a pistol out in front of his haggis. The weapon was aimed at no one in particular, but it was nevertheless prominently displayed.

"What are you men doing here?" Captain Merriwether said. "This is Deirdre territory."

"Not no more," said one of the invaders.

"How'd they get out of the D line?" said a Deirdre.

"Weren't much of a cave-in," said another of the interlopers. "So we dug 'er out. Use more sticks next time," he added, working in the barb.

Perkins aimed his empty pistol at the nearest haggis in the 'lock and hollered, "You men have no business here. Get out now or I'll shoot you where you stand." Bemis likewise held his empty pistol at the ready. It was a well played bluff on their part, but a bluff through and through nevertheless.

"Not if I shoots you first," said the man with the pistol.

"Look around," said Lang. "You're outgunned, mate."

Having looked around, the first man said, "We expected most a ya'd be dead, thanks ta Johnny." Then, "What's goin' on here?" He swept an arm over the piles of supplies, then exclaimed, "Lord, what's the matter with him?" He pointed at the pressure suit playing host to the chickens. It lay uneasily alongside of Mister Lang, writhing and jerking as if whoever or whatever was inside of it was caught in the throes of an epileptic fit. I was about to say that the man had the bubonic plague, or some other notorious pestilence, just to see what effect the news might bring, but Captain Merriwether spoke first.

"Chickens," he said, with a rich disdain.

"They's all suited up," said another of the invaders. "Why're they—"

"Cuz Black Johnny done it!" said the gunman in triumph. "Di'n't kill 'em all outright, but still he done it. Wrecked their engine, don'cha see. That's why there's no lights, and they's all wearin' their gear." Then, "What've ya done with him then, ya thievin' barstards? Where's our Johnny?"

"He's dead," said the captain. "Blew himself to atoms, and the Deirdre with him, damn his eyes."

"Told ya he done it. An' they kilt him for it, ya see."

"Get out now or I promise you I'll shoot," insisted Perkins, running his bluff again.

"Not afore I shoot you," came the response.

Sensing weakness in our opponent, I decided to try turning Perkins's bluff on its head.

"Go on and get out now," I said with a casual insouciance, as if the invading men were a pack of bothersome pups gamboling through my kitchen. "You can't fool us. There's no bullets in that gun."

The silence that ensued was just long enough to constitute a tell, but not quite long enough to make the diagnosis certain. "Hell there ain't," the man said at last, and I knew then that his gun was as empty as the two of ours.

"Shoot me then," barked Perkins, getting into the spirit of the thing. Clearly, he was as convinced of the pistol's impotence as I.

"No, you shoot me first," the man insisted. This deathless exchange was too much for me, and before I could check myself I laughed out loud, ruining the fun.

"Get out!" shouted Perkins, and like Bemis had done with Black Jonny, he threw the empty gun at the man's head. It struck him dead on the money—he was only about a dozen feet away—and rebounded into the Christmas presents. Simultaneously, a crooked star of cracks spread across the man's faceplate.

He took no time to consider, but straight away descended into panic. The pistol fell from his glove, and he said, his voice quavering, "You done it now. Air's no good in here, is it? Deadly, most like. You gone an' kilt me, ya barstards." Black Johnny had infected the lot of them with his distinctive style of profanity, I decided.

"Go back to the Hammer 'n' Tongs then, and good riddance," said Mister Lang.

"Oh Lord, I kin smell the rotten air," the man whined.

"Quit yer bellyachin', Bob," said another of the men. "You ain't dying. Put some patching compound on it." He gestured at the heaps of gear. "There's bound to be plenty in all this junk." Bob did as he was told, and the other man, whom I took to be their leader, turned back to us and said, "We ain't goin' nowhere. Hammer 'n' Tongs ain't producin' like she used to, so we mean to have the Deirdre. Black Johnny explained it to us plenty a times. Said it's ours by right, clear an' legal, once you gone and jumped our claim."

"A madman, a jonah, and a sea lawyer to boot," said Captain Merriwether.

"We didn't intend to jump your claim," Lang said.

Their leader just snorted at that.

"Not that it's any of your business," said the captain, "but as it happens the Deirdre is played out."

"Played out, huh," said the invader. His tone was skeptical, like the man who, although he may be unable to prove it, is still pretty certain that the child isn't his. "A course you're gonna say it's played out, aren't ya? Nossir. That dog won't hunt. You'd best try again." I could almost see the wry, contemptuous smile on his face.

"Why else would we be abandoning her then?" insisted Merriwether, gesturing at the Christmas heap.

"Black Johnny blew up yer engine is why. Can't work the Deirdre without yer engine." I could just make out his grin behind his faceplate. "But we can."

"Think what you like then," Merriwether growled. "You can all of you go straight to the devil. Now stand aside."

There was a moment of quiet, then the leader said, "We'll have your supplies and your spare gear in any case."

"The hell you will," said Lang, raising himself off the vacuum jerky. "There's more of us than there are of you."

"It would be a mercy to shoot us if you intend to take the supplies," mumbled Mister Lovelace. "Without air and water we're as good as dead."

"Start puttin' it in the 'lock, boys," their leader said, then turned to add, "You'd best not try to stop us. There's plenty more men outside the 'lock, you know."

"How're they fixed for bullets?" said Perkins, reaching for a stout length of pipe, and I sensed Mister Lang eyeing the bundle containing Mister Kent's knives.

"Oh dear," murmured Kent.

It looked to me, and no doubt to everyone else present, as if a major donnybrook was about to ensue. It was the predictable end to such a standoff, I suppose, and is certainly the perennial favorite course of action amongst young men in conflict everywhere else I have ever been. The assembled Deirdres did indeed outnumber the men in the airlock, and likely still would after adding in any others that might be waiting their turn outside it. And yet, it seemed equally as obvious to me that no one there had much of an appetite for the project, not even the intrepid Mister Perkins, and I knew perfectly well why. In the end, success at such an enterprise could only be gauged by comparing the magnitude of each side's destruction. If your side punched more holes in, or otherwise seriously damaged, more of the other side's haggises than the other side did of yours, then you were the winner, even if the victors were as full of holes as a colander and dying from asphyxiation. I was feeling very fond of my haggis about then, and I didn't welcome any sort of shenanigans, however noble and steeped in glory they might be, that threatened to derail its crucial mission of keeping me alive. I expect everyone else, with the possible exception of the late Black Johnny Jones, saw things in more or less the same way. Nevertheless, it seemed little short of a certainty that we would all soon come to blows. But as it happened, I had a different idea, and I reckoned there was nothing to be lost in trying it, except my reputation for veracity.

"Captain," I said, with a mighty, if wholly feigned, resignation, "it's no use. That Black Johnny licked us, licked us good, even if he did go to his maker in doin' it." This caused confused, disgruntled grumbling amongst the Deirdres, but I ignored it and steamed ahead. "Just tell them the truth and we can get away from here."

"Shut your gob, Clemens," growled Perkins, and I wondered if he had divined my intentions, or if he simply wanted me to stop talking on general principles.

"Let him speak," said the lead invader.

So I said, "I don't suppose you stopped to examine the rock we'd blasted out right before you came barging into the D line?" I knew full well they hadn't. And they did too.

"What about it?" said the leader.

"Clemens!" hollered Perkins, and an instant later he lunged at me, his gloved hands clutching at my throat, which looked impressive, even if we both knew that the organ he sought was entirely beyond his reach. I decided to add playacting to Perkins's already long list of useful abilities. Captain Merriwether and Bemis added to the show by stepping forward to pummel me, uselessly, about the haggis. All they needed to do to silence me was yank the air hose out of my regulator, or any of a dozen other things that would have put a quick and ugly end to my ravings, but it's the drama that makes the performance, don't you know, and a clutch of fellows punching and kicking a man from every side makes for far better drama, and in this case far less actual injury, than any of them. Besides, if my scheme was performing up to expectations, the men of the Hammer 'n' Tongs would be so pleased that the attack on me was ineffective that they wouldn't stop to consider why that was.

"There's no ice in that rock, it's true," I began, trying to sound as put upon as I looked. Calvin was directly in front of me, and as his gloved fists bounced harmlessly off my partially inflated chest, I caught a glimpse of the grin beyond his faceplate. None of the Deirdres likely had any idea what I was up to, not even Bemis, but to their great credit, they had faith in my well-known ability to confabulate, and were likewise enjoying their part in the play.

"But what there is," I said then, "is heavy metals."

"Clemens, you're a dead man," Perkins spat.

"Iron by the ton, I expect," I continued. "And gold."

"Gold?" two of the invaders said together, with equal parts avarice and awe.

"Nuggets as big as your thumb," I said, throwing caution, but hopefully not all credibility, to the wind.

"Why do you betray us?" moaned the captain, plunging further into the act. "Have we not been good to you? Treated you fairly?"

I remembered Black Johnny's antics then, and prepared to hurl myself into the role like I was Wilkes Booth himself hamming it up in his latest moving picture.

Then a skeptical-sounding Chalk said, "Well now, I been in that line plenty, an' I don't recall any—" Unlike Perkins and the others, he must have slept through the first act.

"Arr, the tyrant Merriwether and his evil henchman Lang," I shouted, stomping smartly on Chalk's inconvenient recollections. "The two a you made the Deirdre a prison, a foul dungeon, a rotten stinking hellhole, where a slow and painful death is the only sure escape." I took a moment to struggle fruitlessly against the Deirdres. "I dares you ta say it ain't so, ya evil barstards." And indeed the captain, Mister Lang, and the others dared not say anything of the kind, not just then, and they continued to beat on me like a drum, presumably to keep the drama up to par. "And these men," I hollered, "these fine upstanding, generous gentlemen—far better than the likes of you, ya barstards—why, they have a working engine."

I threw off my attackers then, with surprising ease, and turned to face my new friends from the Hammer 'n' Tongs. "So I'll join up with you men," I declared smugly. This brought only silence, and a few more half-hearted blows from the amateur thespians. "I'll show you right where it is, too, I will. And I only expects what's rightfully comin' to me in return. An equal share is all I ask, maybe a nugget or two more for my trouble. Nothing extravagant."

The lead invader laughed, as I'd hoped he would. "Go ta hell, mister. What do we want with you? Went an' told us everything we needs ta know, now didn't ya." And he laughed again. "Come on, boys. Let's go dig us some gold." And with that the four men turned, opened the outer hatch, and, the foul wind of the Deirdre's ruined air at their backs, ran off to find their fortunes in gold.

There was no gold in the D line of course, but then there were no additional miners waiting outside the airlock either, so by my calculations we were even.

The eleven of us stood motionless, seemingly afraid that the slightest perturbations would somehow undo our bizarre deliverance. At last someone tried to break the silence with what I believe was to be my name, but he was immediately silenced by Mister Lang. "Don't make a sound," he whispered. "Not 'til we're sure they've gone."

Perkins, obeying Lang's admonition, mimed something to the effect of "I'll trail them for a while, at a safe distance" and went through the now wide-open airlock. A light breeze of highly questionable atmosphere still blew through it, ruffling the hammocks.

When Perkins was gone, Merriwether gestured for us to disable our radios, then drew Bemis, Garrett, and myself to him, so that we could touch our helmets together and talk. Unbidden, Chalk put his helmet against mine.

"Clemens," our former captain said, once helmets had been assembled, "I'm pleased to see that we finally found a use for that rogue tongue of yours. But it won't last. They'll be back here before long, and hopping mad no doubt."

"Particularly at me," I said.

"No doubt," agreed the captain. "I expect we could take them, given our superior numbers— always assuming they don't have another box of shells stowed somewhere—but I see no point in such a fight. Men would end up injured or dead, and valuable gear destroyed, even if we were victorious. So we shall apportion the supplies as best we can, load up the sleds, and take our leave of the Deirdre as soon as possible."

"There's quite a lot of useful, and salable, machinery yet to be salvaged," came a voice, which I soon recognized as that of Mister Lovelace. He must have risen and found a place for his helmet in the scrum. "The engine is certainly destroyed, to my infinite regret, but the valves, fittings, gauges, pipes, tubing, and the like in the belowdecks alone—"

"Quite right, Mister Lovelace," said the captain. "I'm pleased to see that you have recovered yourself sufficiently to return to your duties. Take Winters, and perhaps Chalk—are you still taking orders from me, Gottschalk?"

"Aye, Cap'n. A course, Cap'n. I only—"

"Fine. Then you and Winters help Mister Lovelace to salvage as much as he can before we're forced to depart. Put whatever you collect in the remaining two ore cars. And mind what Mister Lovelace tells you. There's no point in hauling out a parcel of trash. Now, off with you."

"Aye," said Chalk and Winters together, and they and Mister Lovelace left the scrum.

"Now, Garrett—are you there?"

"Yessir," Garrett said.

"Good. You and Watkins go and get your machine ready to travel. You'll need some water." He gestured at a pile of containers. "Inform myself or Mister Lovelace immediately if you encounter any difficulties. Without your digger's resonance engine performing properly, we are as good as pooped. Mister Bemis, I trust you can do the same for your machine. Clemens can assist you, or else start hauling out supplies. You men will need water and other goods, but it's not possible to say how much you're likely to need without knowing where it is you're going. Do you have a destination, Mister Bemis?" It was clear from his tone that Merriwether thought we were making a mistake to go off on our own.

"Not at the moment," Calvin admitted.

"Mister Clemens?"

I said, "I think we should consult Mister Perkins before we decide."

"That would be wise, I expect," Merriwether agreed. "In the meantime, Mister Lang and I will try to determine as exactly as possible how much water, grub, and other kit we will need to get nine men safely to Lucky Strike. What remains of the supplies is yours. If it is not sufficient—" I sensed a shrug. "—then what course you steer after that is up to you."

"Here's Perkins now," said Bemis.

Perkins instantly grasped the situation and joined the scrum.

"They appear to have bought Clemens's story, at least for the moment," he said. "They were quite a distance into the D line by the time I started back."

"Very good," Merriwether said. "I believe we can reactivate the radios then." We all did so, and Merriwether continued directing the evacuation.

It was decided that, while Calvin worked to revive the Beast, and Mister Lang and the captain divvied up the supplies, Perkins and I should assemble the tents the two parties would require for their respective journeys, secure each to the appropriate conveyance, such as a sled or a parade float, inflate same, and outfit them with the supplies and other gear that each would need. This was a formidable task, but it appealed to me, or my pride anyway. As the reader may recall, my first bout with a vacuum tent—so very long ago it seemed by then—had been decided overwhelmingly in favor of the tent. The way I saw it, I had the right to a rematch, and with Mister Perkins in my corner, I felt certain that this time I should emerge victorious, or at least manage a draw.

Chapter Thirteen

I hadn't thought to ask what conditions were like out on the surface just then, or to put it another way, what time of day it happened to be. It seemed like years since I'd last seen the stars, and fully an age since I'd been in the presence of His Majesty the Sun. I did not much regret my hiatus from the latter, however, for on the Moon he is not at all the benign presence he appears to be when one lives on Earth. There, he is a gentle, benevolent, and, dare I say it, enlightened monarch (except perhaps in the more forlorn deserts). But out in the Mare Imbrium or the Montes Caucuses, where one is exposed to his full fire and fury, he is a tyrant, and not an amusing tyrant like King Kamehameha or Louis XIV either, but a genuine, old-fashioned crucifixion-and-scorched-earth character in the mold of Caligula, Ivan the Terrible, or Attila the Hun, eager to burn out your eyes with his light, strip the skin from your flesh with his searing heat, and slowly but steadily poison your insides with penetrating torrents of invisible radiation.

But like any man of the modern age, I thought such despots a phenomenon of the distant past, or if extant, then confined to backward and dreary lands such as the Belgian Congo or Canada. Therefore, I loped innocently up the main tunnel leading to the surface, and only stopped to consider what had become of my sun shield when I caught a glimpse of eye-searing white beyond the tunnel's mouth. When I reached the opening, close behind Perkins, who held the other end of my burden, and Bemis, who carried two twenty-gallon containers of water ice weighing a total of about fifty pounds, I saw that the Sun was low on the horizon, which caused the seven hills of tailings to cast long coal-black shadows across the otherwise scorched regolith, all seven of them pointing in our direction. Incidentally, there was no advantage in it being sunset or sunrise, except that one could escape the tyrant's wrath by ducking into the shadows—otherwise the Sun's rays are just as lethal at sunset as they are at high noon.

"Is it sunrise or sunset?" I asked no one in particular, since as far as I was concerned there was no way to tell the difference.

But Perkins answered me immediately with, "It's sunrise, I regret to say."

"How can you tell?" I insisted, turning away from the vista of the seven hills before I lost my eyesight to it.

"It's a matter of the direction," he said, clarifying nothing.

"The direction of what?"

"Why, the Sun of course, ya silly booger. If it's in front of us here, then it must be rising."

"I see," I said, which of course I didn't. "And how do you know that?" I added, still hoping to get to the bottom of the matter.

"Because I've been here for going on two years now, and so I've seen it a time or two."

Hopes dashed, I postponed that line of enquiry until I could corner an astronomer, or else a practicing druid who could align the Sun between the mounds of tailings and predict how many weeks of winter remained.

I tried Bemis instead. "Calvin, where did we leave our sun shields?"

"They're in the digger's cabin," he answered immediately.

The Beast was resting, otherwise exactly as we had left him months ago, half in and half out of the shadow of one of the seven hills, but a distance of forty yards separated the tunnel's mouth from that protecting shadow. It helped not a bit that the Sun was shining—a word that describes the true ferocity of the tyrant's gaze about as well as a trout dances the two-step—directly into our faceplates.

"I've secured mine," said Perkins. I had been behind him for the whole journey out of the Deirdre, and therefore hadn't noticed. "I'll rouse them out of your machine and bring them to you here."

"That seems a waste of your time, and ours," said Calvin. "Sam and I will hold our hands over our faceplates and you can lead us across to the shadow. Then I'll retrieve the shields."

Perkins agreed to this and, gloves held firmly to our faces, we stepped into the full fierce light of day. Since we were now sightless, and scurrying across the roasting surface with Perkins nudging us along by the elbows, I thought it fitting to offer up a chorus or two of the "Three Blind Mice" to pass the time. But, although Perkins seemed to take the entertainment in stride, Bemis uttered my name in such a disgusted tone that I soon felt disabused of the notion and ceased.

Once in the blessed shade, we were permitted sight again—although, like a parson who wanders into a peep show, I had to take great care in where I directed my gaze. Calvin leapt onto the Beast, climbed rapidly up its great orange flank, worked open the Dutch oven, and got inside. Meanwhile Perkins and I, staying carefully in the shade, reattached the sled and unrolled one of the vacuum tents upon it. This article was not at all the puny little blister we had occupied so ignominiously on the trip out. Even lying in uninflated repose, it filled the entire sled, which caused me to wonder where we were to put the supplies. That tent was in fact the deluxe model, a capacious half-cylinder with room enough to accommodate four men, or two men and their haggises, or, as we soon discovered, one man, two haggises, and a brood of angry hens.

"How is it that the Deirdre has such a fine collection of vacuum tents?" I asked.

"There wasn't always the belowdecks and such, you know. We lived in them while we dug out the mine."

"Of course," I said.

"Rented one of your diggers for that," he added. Then, before I could say a word to stop him, he attached an air cylinder to a valve and turned the cock to start the process of filling the tent with air.

I stood mute while the tent grew larger and took on its true shape and dimensions, only chuckling audibly two or three times. But finally I could stand it no longer and said, "Well, you've done it now, Mister Perkins," and I chuckled again.

He said, "If we're going to be partners, then you ought to call me Lawrence, don't you think."

"Well, Lawrence,"—I knew I'd have to improve on that unwieldy handle somehow—"I see you have gone and sacrificed a cylinder of good air. Don't feel too bad about it though, Bemis and I made precisely the same mistake on the trip out."

"What are you talking about, Clemens?"

"Please, Lawrence, call me Sam," I said, feeling magnanimous. "You've left us no way in that doesn't get rid of all the air in the process."

I waited patiently for him to say 'booger me', or some variation of it, but instead he laughed and said, "Where did you get that idea? Come look at this," and he led me around to one end of the half-cylinder. I saw immediately that there was an extra piece of material attached to the flat side, with a slit down its middle big enough, if only barely, to admit a man in a pressure suit.

Bemis arrived with my sun shield then, and I slipped it over my faceplate and dogged the corners down to keep it securely in place.

"Is that an airlock?" I said, knowing it must be so, but at the same time knowing nothing about how it might work.

"Yes, of a sort," said Perkins. "I'll show you how it operates in due course. For now, we'd best start stowing our kit."

The rest of the Deirdres came out of the mine's entrance about then, some of them carrying huge bundles of supplies, and the rest pushing or pulling the two remaining ore carts, now loaded with spare parts and whatever items of value they could strip from the belowdecks and the galley, including the captain's desk and Mister Kent's iron cookstove. All of them wore sun shields, since as it happened Mister Lovelace actually knew what time of day it was, through the miracle of his owning a working pocket watch, as well as the brains to know how to use it, and he had warned the captain about the rising sun in time for him to dig the shields out of the Christmas heap.

As he lay in the shade of one of the hills, rightly coddling his wounded limb, Mister Lang directed us in the decommissioning of the dust boat. We tore the aluminum sheeting from the vehicle, dismantled the frame that supported it, then used a portion of the sheeting to improvise a second sled in which to carry our supplies. I was sorry to see the end of the dust boat, it had after all been the instrument of our salvation, and by my lights it deserved a bow of the helmet and a moment of silence prior to its destruction. But the Deirdres seemed to feel nothing for the singular craft and tore it limb-from-limb with unsentimental efficiency. For better or worse, its time had come to an end. Future greenhorns stranded in Farley's Crater would have to wait on a host of winged chariots or a canoe full of red Indians for their rescue from there on out.

The party intent upon returning to civilization had a surfeit of men, and they rapidly set the second tent atop the naked parade float, introduced it to Garrett's fine, if inferior, digging leviathan, then attached another makeshift sled to their train. With that completed, we were ready for the gear and supplies to be loaded, and much care was taken in their sharing out between the two parties, according to a scheme based upon both the size of each company and, in the case of the larger, the time estimated to complete the journey to Lucky Strike. The water was given the closest attention, naturally, followed by the air cylinders, and then the food. Perkins handled the negotiations for the newly-reconstituted Clemens-Bemis Expedition, as we thought his superior knowledge, when coupled with his relentlessly pugnacious manner, might serve to prevent the Merriwether Party from hogging precious supplies. And our faith was not misplaced, as even his old friend Percy Lang was called a wily booger once or twice over the distribution of the remaining air.

As to the food, I offered to forgo the entire store of vacuum jerky in exchange for one dented but otherwise serviceable can of pickled beets, but my trade was vetoed by Calvin, who had somehow acquired a taste for jerky—much like a misguided missionary who spends too much time with cannibals and develops a taste for long pig. After that, the only articles of grub still to be distributed were busy fouling Captain Merriwether's spare pressure suit, and their disposition was a conundrum. Divvying the chickens up amongst the two parties would mean dragging the haggis full of hens in and out of both tent's airlocks, costing each a small but not inconsiderable amount of valuable air each time. And in addition, Mister Kent reminded us that any hens deprived of their cock would surely pine for the execrable bird and cease to lay, or worse, simply expire from ennui. The captain declared that they would all die of vacuum poisoning if it were left to him, and in the end the wriggling haggis full of poultry was awarded to the Clemens-Bemis company in exchange for an armload of, yes, vacuum jerky. Perkins was skeptical of the transaction, but I thought it an excellent trade, which only serves to illustrate my keen lack of foresight, as well as my loathing for jerky in any and all of its forms.

The steam-powered tractor that had been at the heart of the dust boat was to be put to work hauling the two ore carts, now laden with all the mechanical detritus Mister Lovelace, Winters, and Chalk had stripped out of the mine. The two parties, minus Bemis and Garrett, who were powering up their respective machines, then set to parceling out the most useful of the spoils, with our party concentrating on parts that might help to repair an injured haggis, or if necessary return the Beast's resonance engine to health.

I was carrying our share of these goods to the sled when I saw a rock fly past my faceplate. Now, that is novelty, I thought. Hens may fly when living in the Moon, but rocks, if left to their own devices, never do.

I turned around to see where the missile could have started from, and saw yet another chunk of regolith coming my way. I managed to duck—not an easy thing whilst carrying a double armload of very awkward junk—but before the stone could get to my immediate vicinity, it struck a protuberance on the side of the Beast and ricocheted up into the black sky, soon traveling high enough to escape the shadow in which I stood and catch the rays of the rising sun. Since it would take most of the afternoon to return to the ground, I dismissed it and turned my attention to the mouth of the mine, where I suspected the flying rocks had originated, and was in time to see three men emerge from the blackness and shuffle cautiously out into the tyrant's fiery stare. Apparently they had misplaced their sun shields, because each wore a hastily improvised substitute; a ragged piece of aluminum atop the helmet served as a sun bonnet, and did quite a poor job of it, I'm sure.

Captain Merriwether, who was busy securing bundles of supplies to his party's sled, shouted, "Deirdres, stay in the sunlight!"

This was good advice, since without proper sun shields the imbeciles from the Hammer 'n' Tongs—for that was surely who they were, come once again to squeeze water, or blood if they could manage it, from the stone that was the Deirdre mine—would be hard pressed to see us in the un-shielded glare, especially as they were forced by their position to stare directly into the horrendous rising Sun.

Still, our standing in the sun did nothing to actually counter the threat.

Another rock came sailing toward me, hurled, I saw, by the occupant of the haggis in the van. His aim was improving with practice, and his latest offering almost struck me. I stopped to drop my load of junk onto the supply sled and considered. That rock had nearly hit the side of our tent on its way to meet me. I reckoned that I might be expendable, all things considered, but the tent surely was not, and a well-placed piece of regolith, equipped with the sharp points and ragged edges so very common to its species, could tear a hole in the fabric that would put a sudden end to our prospecting plans.

Perkins of course was way ahead of me in his thinking, and miles beyond me in courage. He leapt from his position on the rear of the Beast, where he had been connecting hoses of some kind from the digger to the tent, snatched up a length of pipe with a nasty, jagged end on it out of my junk pile, and barked, "Sam, grab something sharp, or at least heavy, and we'll have a go at them. Our sun shields should give us the advantage."

I looked around hurriedly. Bemis was in the cabin of the digger, persuading it back to life, so the company's defense was apparently up to me. I drew a pickaxe—a Clemens-Bemis Expedition pickaxe—from the supplies sled, stepped out of the shade into the blinding horizontal sun, and hopped in the general direction of the foe, with Perkins out ahead of me, and no idea what I was aiming to do, as usual.

Along with the stones, there were plenty of curses flying through the aether by then, and a dozen men shouting into their radios to no good purpose. I found that I was being encouraged, although not accompanied, I noticed, by the men of the captain's party, and repeatedly identified as an "evil barstard" by our attackers. From them there was also much talk of lying, of which I was surely guilty, but also of thievery, of which I was not, as far as I could remember.

It took less than a minute for Perkins and myself to close with the three marauders, which on the one hand was a problem for me, because I was not ready for battle—a statement that I suspect will always be true enough—and on the other a blessing, because I didn't have time to come to my senses and run away.

Perkins's charge was so fierce and swift that his man waddled backwards at his approach and nearly fell over himself in his haste to regain the mouth of the tunnel. Perkins of course pursued him, and soon disappeared into the mine, leaving me to deal with the other two by myself. I planted my boots a few yards in front of the first of the men, whom I strongly suspected was the smart-mouthed leader of these determined, doggedly persistent, and deeply stupid men. I brandished my pickaxe, and speaking quite loudly to cut through the cursing and other caterwauling, said, "Give it up, man. You'll get nothing but a punctured haggis for your trouble, I can guarantee it."

"What?" he said, then growled, "Fuck you, mate," and swung a shovel at my helmet, something that nearly everyone around there seemed to like to do. Fortunately, my pickaxe was almost in the path of the swing, and I was able to put it in the way in time to deflect the blow. There was no sound from the impact of shovel against axe of course, but a numbing vibration traveled up my arm, and I nearly dropped my weapon. A spirited, very dangerous, and essentially pointless pick and shovel fight then ensued—exactly the sort of destruction we all, or at least the Deirdres, had wished to avoid.

Although the two weapons were nearly as light as a couple of feathers due to the low gravity, they were also extremely hard to direct accurately with arms encased in inflated canvas tubes. I raised my axe and swung at the man with gusto, and missed him by the better part of a mile. The substantial mass of the axe, which did not it appeared depart with the weight, kept it moving where it wanted to go, and I found myself spun around by its momentum until I'd traveled through most of a complete circle. Definitely too much gusto, I thought. I blocked another blow to the helmet and prepared to swing again, when I noticed that Chalk had come calling, wielding a length of pipe with a huge angry-looking gauge at the business end. He was hopping back and forth in front of the other man, waving the pipe shillelagh over his head like the crazed Leprechaun he was.

His man held a knife, and a fearsome one too, by the look of it, a long stout blade with a wicked serrated edge. This was a weapon of substance, one far more deadly to a man in a pressure suit than any number of shovels and pickaxes. Chalk, whom I had suspected of being shy when it came to a fight—a sentiment I generally approve of—nevertheless got in the first lick, a stunning blow to the helmet that served to knock away the man's sun bonnet, if nothing else. Chalk's blow had been too much for his makeshift shillelagh, however, and the big gauge that adorned its end broke off and hurled itself away. Besides that, it was quite a healthy shot, and its force lifted Chalk ten or twelve feet off the ground. The foe, for his part, staggered backwards upon its receipt and, crucially for us, lost his grip on that ugly knife.

I swung my axe at my opponent again, summoning up considerably less gusto this time, and was rewarded with a yelp of pain, or at least surprise, as the blade's edge struck the arm of his suit. Meanwhile, Chalk made a dive for the knife, which lay on the ground between him and its erstwhile owner. He fell within reach of the weapon and was about to take it up, when his opponent, who had recovered somewhat from Chalk's shillelagh, stepped forward and kicked him squarely in the head, or rather the helmet. It was hard to say who got the worst part of that exchange, but the feline howl that came through the radio left me with no doubt as to Puss's opinion. For his part, Chalk was stunned into immobility, but for every blow offered there is (I am told) an equal and opposite blow delivered to he who initiated the fun, and the man duly roared in pain. (I don't know how one is supposed to win a fight at all under such rules, since according to the savants each man will get exactly as good as he gives from now until doomsday. Perhaps it is a matter of where one lands the blows.)

I turned back to face my own foe, wondering for an instant why he hadn't clobbered me while I was distracted by Chalk's plight. It seemed that my blow had had a greater effect than I had expected, and I saw that the glove of the man's weapon arm was now empty, and his other glove was pressed over the spot I had struck, whether to soothe the pain of it, or to stanch the flow of air from a tear in his haggis, I could not say. It occurred to me then that I was the only gladiator in the arena still possessed of a weapon, and I thought of simply declaring victory, departing the field, and awaiting my triumph in the comfort of my tent, like a Roman general plundering his way through Gaul.

Alas, I had not counted on the popularity of that knife. Chalk and his man were soon engaged in a vigorous struggle for its possession, each trying to grasp some part of the weapon that would not result in the shredding of their gloves, like a fox attempting to negotiate with a porcupine, and I decided I ought to weigh in, presumably on Chalk's behalf, before someone got hurt. But how, I wondered, there were already more gloves in the vicinity of that knife than the traffic would bear. Then I had it. I tossed the axe behind me—it rebounded after striking the prow of the Beast and nearly returned itself to me—then I picked up my adversary's shovel and delivered a smart blow to the helmet on everyone within range, except Chalk, although I admit I was tempted to make a clean sweep.

The first blow, which I served up to the man battling for possession of the knife, set him staggering, and left me several feet off the ground, as striking downward is liable to send the blow's deliverer in the opposite direction. The view was better from that height, and I was able to deliver to my original opponent a blow to the crown of his shining brass helmet that left him on the ground, too stunned even to curse effectively. Of course this second blow propelled me nearly into orbit, a result I should have anticipated but somehow did not, and although the view was impressive from up there, I found that I had managed to remove myself from the festivities just when I might be needed most. Fortunately, I was still facing away from the raging sun and toward the mine entrance, and thus as I fell back to the surface I saw Perkins emerge from the black maw of the Deirdre mine, hopping eagerly toward the three stunned figures below me. I say three because Chalk appeared just as incapacitated as the other two, and without my help.

As it happened, Puss had also been vying for Chalk's attention, as I learned when I heard him grumble, "Argh. Puss, dear, this is no time to be havin' a piss." Considering all that had recently transpired, my sympathies were wholly with Puss in the matter.

As I returned to the ground, I examined the surrounding regolith, but could see no sign of the dreaded but much-coveted knife. That was because, while everyone else stood stunned, and I floated in the aether, Perkins had run in and scooped up the prize. An instant later he stood poised before the two hostiles, the tip of the weapon pointing first at one man then the other, sniffing the vacuum for fresh blood like it was Lucifer's own divining rod.

"Now, you two ugly boogers," Perkins barked, "go back in the tunnel with the others and stay there, else I'll carve you up like a pair of prize hogs." There was something unmistakable in his tone that promised he was telling the truth.

"What you done with Bob?" said one of the miscreants, with what I considered stunning irrelevance.

Nevertheless Perkins answered him. "After I busted his lamp, he run away, the sorry booger. I expect he's got himself good and lost by now." He took a step forward. "Now get moving or I'll have no choice but to kill you both." I raised the shovel in solidarity.

The two men stood there in silence, each holding up a hand to shield his faceplate and considering

Perkins's proposition. At last convinced of his veracity, they turned and began to shuffle toward the mine. Then a moment later one of them said, "Well, Bob, there you be. Good a you ta join us."

Perkins, whose back was to the mine, laughed, saying, "Nice try, boys, but—"

"No!" I hollered, but my warning came too late, and Bob, who had launched himself from the tunnel in a low but rapid trajectory, fell on Perkins from behind—quite literally fell on top of him in fact—and held fast to the twin air cylinders on Perkins's back.

Perkins spun around—a largely useless gesture when your opponent is riding you piggy-back, as I had discovered for myself whilst aboard Black Johnny. I saw the two men who had been retreating toward the mine's entrance turn, place hands over faceplates, and contemplate a return to the arena. I stepped toward them and raised the shovel in order to hold them at bay. Then, grasping the nature of his predicament, Perkins reached behind him with the awful knife and tried to slash at his rider. The knife struck hard against the man's helmet, spun out of Perkins's glove, and flew on into the shadow cast by a mountain of tailings. I repeat, it's best to go light on the gusto when involved in hand-to-hand combat on the Moon.

Chalk, who had recovered somewhat from the repeated blows to his helmet, if not Puss's ministrations, ran to retrieve the wicked blade.

Meanwhile, Perkins continued to flail about, trying to dislodge his rider by the time-honored method of bucking him off, a trick that has worked more than once on me, generally through the offices of a genuine Mexican plug. But despite Perkins's best efforts, the man stayed in the saddle, although honestly I'm not at all sure what he was trying to accomplish. It had done me little good against Black Johnny.

Then Chalk returned, holding the knife out in front of him, acting like he wished to give it to Perkins, who already had his hands full wrestling with his jockey.

"Chalk!" shouted Perkins, "cut his air hose!"

Presumably to this end, Chalk then hopped up and attached himself to Perkins's rider's back. This is beginning to resemble a circus act, I thought, or perhaps a cannibal bride's three-tiered wedding cake. Just how many men in full pressure regalia could Perkins hold, I wondered, and nearly considered climbing aboard myself in order to find out.

The question was soon answered without me, however, when, as Chalk tried to aim the knife while riding two bucking haggises, Perkins lost his balance and began to pitch forward, falling in slow motion. Naturally, both the rider and the rider's rider came along to fall on top of him. I heard a scream, and simultaneously was witness to a horrible sight, as a huge geyser of air erupted from somewhere within the pile of pressure-suited men. The dreaded knife had done its work, and one of the men in that fateful scrum was now on a swift passage to perdition. But which was it? Since Chalk had held the knife when the tower fell—hadn't he?—the odds said that Perkins's attacker was the victim, but as often happens when I dare to gamble, the odds were wrong. Just as the toast invariably falls butter side down, it was Perkins, not his attacker, who was spouting a geyser of air.

"All right," came a voice I knew well, but somehow didn't expect to hear, "that's about enough of that. Sam, can you get Perkins into the airlock?" The voice was that of Calvin Bemis.

"Which airlock?" I said, grabbing Perkins and hoisting him off the ground. His haggis was hopelessly flaccid, all the air having escaped through a terrible rent in its side. Then, as I glanced toward the mine's entrance to see what had become of the other men, I saw the elongated shadow of a set of monstrous jaws reach ahead of me across the ground.

"Get out of the way, Sam," shouted Bemis, and I knew then what was happening. Calvin had summoned the Beast, if not to its rightful work, then in service to a righteous cause. The shadow advanced on the attackers and, as I dragged Perkins's limp haggis aside, I saw the great digging leviathan roll inexorably past, pursuing the three men, its huge digging claw outstretched and its spiked jaws open wide.

One of the foe made the mistake of turning to see exactly what sort of nightmare was pursuing him. He was immediately blinded by the Sun, of course, and stood with his gloves over his faceplate as Bemis scooped him up in the Beast's claw like a sinner raised up by the hand of God—or perhaps the hand of the other fellow. Then Calvin swung the claw and tossed the man away into the vacuum, where he sailed majestically over all seven hills of tailings and beyond. I expect he did come down, eventually, somewhere over the eastern horizon.

Epilogue

Well, Calvin and I didn't die in the Deirdre either, although it was not for lack of trying. Instead, we took the expanded Clemens-Bemis Expedition into the Vallis Alpes, where, as you might imagine, some additional trouble occurred. To find out just what sort of trouble, you will need to read Mark Twain on the Moon Book Three, available soon wherever fine books are sold.

Please visit michaelschulkins.com for more information, as well as special offers on other books in the Mark Twain on the Moon series.

Made in the USA
Middletown, DE
25 April 2019